FSC
www.fsc.org
MIX
Papier aus ver-
antwortungsvollen
Quellen
Paper from
responsible sources
FSC® C105338

AF190280

In 2015 I started a series of fetish-thrillers for German speaking people. Now I publish the first story of that series in English. I'm curious to see where it will lead to.

My publisher says very clearly, that translations should be done by professional translators that have to speak English as mother tongue. I'm no professional translator and I learned English as second language.

Nevertheless, I wanted to give it a try. Yes, I have to confess that, somewhere in my mind, I thought I would endure maybe 50 pages. But I had so much fun in translating my book, that I just did it until the last page.
I didn't imagine how many homonyms my language has. The internet-translators often pick the wrong meaning. As I said: Very funny.

I'm sure the pages you get as book sample will give you an idea whether my translations are rubbish or okay. I promise that I have paid the same attention to the entire translation.

Hope you enjoy the story

Gabriel Erbé

https://gabrielerbe.jimdo.com

Gabriel Erbé
A strange blackmail

A fetish-thriller

From German by Gabriel Erbé

Bibliografische Information der Deutschen Nationalbibliothek. Die Deutsche Nationalbibliothek verzeichnet diese Publikation in der Deutschen Nationalbibliografie; detaillierte bibliografische Daten sind im Internet über www.dnb.de abrufbar.

| Manufacturer and publisher: | BoD – Books on Demand - Norderstedt |

The original edition was published by BoD in 2015 under the title *Eine seltsame Erpressung*

© 2019 Gabriel Erbé

ISBN 9-783750-426177

Prolog

Several ropes looped around her body. Her arms were tied together on her back, so she had to grab the elbow of the left arm with her right hand and the other way around. Her upper body and thighs formed a straight line. The lower legs were pulled up to the thighs. An eyelet hung down from the high ceiling on a chain. On the ropes surrounding her thigh, her waist, and her chest, there were more ropes attached that led to that eyelet. Since the young woman had no contact with the ground, she swung very slowly around her own axis and looked full of pleasure into the camera.

„One more lap, my dear and you are redeemed."

She threw her head back, causing the rope to swing gently. One last time she could enjoy the indescribable feeling of hanging on the rope safely and helplessly at the same time.

A short time later, the photographer came to her and slowly lowered her to the floor, where he undid the ropes one after the other.

„You were great again. I do not understand how you can stand this for so long."

„You're just a real bondage master, Marc. I have never experienced a bondage artist who can spread the weight of my body on the ropes as well as you do."

„Well…" As always Marc could not really handle the praise. To her delight, he blushed and preferred not to go further into his art.

„Have a coffee or whatever you want. If that's okay with you, then we continue with the stainless-steel cuffs in half an hour."

He held out a bathrobe for her.

„And quickly slip into this. You know that I'm always scared that my models might catch a cold when they go out of the warm spotlight after a shoot with all the sweat on their beautiful bodies."

She took the bathrobe with a grateful smile and went into the small lounge next to the studio.

She was very curious how the next shoot would be. So far, she had always only had photos made, on which her body was artfully tied with ropes. The stainless-steel bands would be a whole new experience for her. As she sat comfortably with a cup of coffee in one of the armchairs and massaged the places where the ropes had been sitting, her eyes wandered across the room. On the table, various photo magazines crisscrossed each other. She could not help but fold them into a proper stack. After that, she would have liked to clean the glass top of the table. Not that it was really dirty. If Marc had tolerated dirt in his studio in addition to the mess in his lounge, she would never have been ready for the shootings. Even so, there were some greasy stains on the glass plate as they occur when you put your hands on the plate. But instead of cleaning she was fascinated by what she saw in the shelf under the table top.

The stainless-steel cuff gleamed as if it had just been freshly polished. It was lined from the inside with a soft black fabric, which looked out over the steel on both sides and offered a wonderful contrast to the shiny stainless steel. She carefully took the part out and examined it more closely. The lock was open and provided with a strong ring which, after closing the cuff, would be used to fasten various restraints. Previously she had always assumed that such cuffs would be closed with a simple padlock. However, this lock would no longer be rec-ognizable as a lock after closing and thus had much more style for her sense of art. If the ring were not so clearly bondage, the whole thing could have been considered an extravagant piece of jewelry.

Right of, she decided to put the cuff around her neck and let the lock snap in. She looked at herself in the wall mirror. She liked what she saw very well. She had no idea why she had not tried that out much earlier.

„My dear, can you continue or do you need more break?"
Marc's voice from the studio had, as always, this particular
questioning undertone.

„I'll be right back!"

She took the last sip of coffee and went back into the studio.
After seeing herself in the mirror, she could hardly wait to
wear more of those wonderful cuffs.

When Marc saw her, his friendly smile froze for a moment.
„Where did you get this nice jewelry from?"

„It was lying on the table." She pointed towards the lounge.
„Shouldn't I have taken that?"

Marc scratched the back of his head. Having worked with
him for a long time, she knew there was some problem.

„My mistake. You know that you can always try everything
that is lying around here. But I should not have left that lying
around."

„What's so special about it, except that it looks great."

He touched his chin.

„Glad you like it, because you'll have to wear it for about a
month now."

She looked at him speechless and then laughed.

„You and your jokes. Let's get started. I can't wait to see
what else you have for me."

She went to the small illuminated stage.

„My dear?" he started carefully.

„Marc, be quiet now and get it started!"

He did not seem quite happy, but then started to put cuffs
on her ankles and wrists. He then showed her a chastity belt
made of the same material and explained how it would be
worn.

„Women, who are a little bit more in this kind of things,
attach even dildos to it. Actually, I can't really imagine that
this is comfortable. Of course, we do it without dildo, right?"

„Of course. But now get it started Marc. That's what I'm
here for. The main thing is, you do not throw the key away",
she joked.

11

Less than an hour later he had chained her in the most varied positions and he had done everything he wanted to do.

„Then I want to redeem you."

After a short time, he had removed everything except the collar and held out her bathrobe. She pointed to her neck

„I think it is really pretty, but if you could remove it too?"

Again, he touched the back of his head.

„I was afraid you did not take me seriously. I really can't open it. I am currently working on a time lock. You have one of my first exemplars around your neck. This morning the mechanism was still locked. I assume it opened automatically during the day. Then you have found the part, put it around your neck and closed it again. In about a month, it will open itself again."

Automatically she pulled on the steel band, which of course did not open. Marc looked at her with a smile that she could not interpret.

„I hope you do not find that funny", she wanted to know.

„Yes, actually. No idea how many of those who come to my shootings dream of getting into such a situation with heart and soul. So, you have a time to be the absolute eye-catcher. That's all. What's the difference?"

„That this could be embarrassing for me is nothing that comes to your mind?"

Marc took a theatrical pose for a short time.

„No, but I still have something equivalent to offer for your wrists and ankles."

„Are you completely crazy now?"

Without a hint of the typical gay tone he always used, he gave a completely unexpected answer.

„If you're that bitchy any longer, then you will leave this studio with such cuffs. I can't help it, that you are so curious. I've given you the opportunity to get out of the number fairly cool long enough. Now I do not feel like it anymore. Get lost."

Saturday 30th April / Sunday 1st May

The waitress came to the couple's table to clear it from the leftovers of the main course.

„Did you enjoy your meal?"

„Are you serious, Miss?"

He did not speak overly loudly, but loud enough to silence the conversations at the neighboring tables.

„The side salad was tasteless and the turkey breast chewy. The rest of the meal was decent."

He turned to his companion.

„How was your meal?"

„I liked it very much."

The waitress thanked with a friendly smile and disappeared with the promise to forward the complaint.

„Carl, the guest at Table 7 judged the salad to be tasteless and the turkey to be chewy."

The cook glared at the waitress.

„What does he think? In fact, he has never had such an excellent meal! Table 7, you said?"

The waitress nodded. The cook only looked briefly through the small spin hole in the door.

„Him again. He wants to ruin me. Give him and his wife schnapps. Serve her a bad and him a good one."

„The woman was very polite the whole evening" protested the waitress.

„Exactly because of that. Just do it. You will see."

The waitress put the two shot glasses in front of their guests.

„The cook asks this as small reparation to accept. Cheers."

„Surely you give my wife the best liquor. She is always so nice and polite. And I got the cheapest shit you could find. Believe me, I know stores like this!"

Before the waitress could open her mouth to protest, he had exchanged the glasses and downed his drink. When his wife saw his face, she took her glass and sipped it once.

„It's perfect. Thanks to the cook", she told the waitress with a friendly smile.

„The bill" came croaking from her counterpart.

When they left the restaurant, Yvonne hooked up with her husband.

„Why do you always think that everyone just wants to be cross with you MM?"

„It must be allowed to complain about the food!"

She looked at him questioningly.

„It really did not taste?"

„The waitress just got on my nerves. I absolutely had to put her in her place."

„Oh MM. She just did her job. And that she does not look like your ideal of beauty, she can not do anything about it."

He gently stroked her hand.

„Probably you are right, my love. We want to finish this topic now."

„In other words, you have no desire to talk about it and do not even understand why one or the other has problems with your conceptions."

„I could not have said it better."

„You are really a hopeless case in such things, MM."

Not for the first time, Yvonne was annoyed that he was reluctant to talk about his mistakes and always dismissed such topics with 'probably you're right' or 'we'll talk about it another time'. When they arrived at the end of the shopping street, MM waved a taxi to take them home.

„Yvonne, my key seems to be broken. Please try yours."

MM wiggled the lock without the key slipping in properly.

„Can it be that the lock just broke MM?"

Yvonne also tried unsuccessfully to insert the key into the lock.

„It would be strange. That has not even been notchy yet. I'll try the side entrance."

A short time later he opened the door from the inside.

„Look at this."

He took her by the hand and pulled her to the cabinet in the lobby. There was a picture of a fully armed comic heroine with an unavoidable dream figure. The caption was:

„I'm sorry about the lock. I've always wanted to push superglue into such a lock. You will get over the loss. Presumably you will forget the loss even in a few seconds, when you have inspected your beautiful little safe."

MM did not get any further. He ran to his study. The image that was supposed to hide the vault stood on the floor. The vault was open and empty. MM dropped heavily onto the desk chair and stared at the vault.

„Oh my god!"

Yvonne stood in the doorway, holding both hands over her mouth.

„You have to call the police. There was a robbery in our house."

He turned to her.

„You're nuts? What was in there is illegal income without exception. You know that. Shall I tell the police that I've been stolen an estimated one million Euro? Illegal one million Euro?"

Yvonne's eyes went wide in sudden panic.

„My jewelry! I hope he did not find my jewelry!"

She was already up the stairs when he answered in a low voice.

„Then we buy new jewelry. No need to get so excited. Women make too much fuss about their jewelry anyway."

Half an hour later, they searched the house, but found no further signs of burglary. The burglar had only cracked the safe and disappeared with its contents.

„What a brazenness to attach such a note to the cabinet. As if he knew exactly that we could not go to the police. Besides, why does he think he can just chatter us? Do we know each other or what is it?"

When there was no answer from his wife, he looked back at her.

„Yvonne, where are you?"

„I'm here, MM. In the hallway. I think you should read the rest of the note as well. That's really a strong piece."

„But you should have a chance to influence your destiny and that of all the printed paper. I figure that we play a little game. Actually, several little games, but more on that later. Here is the first game:

Wanted is a city that you should visit today. I can assume that midnight is already over? So, you both have time. Finally, it's Sunday. The game is not really hard, because I give the coordinates of the building, where I expect you at noon: 50° 56' 26" N, 6° 57' 30" E"

MM looked at Yvonne thoroughly aghast.

„He seriously has the idea that we drive around in the world, just because he wants. He should forget that idea as soon as possible. I'm not going to start dancing to the tune of some stupid thief. As soon as I've caught him, I'll destroy him and his jamming belongings. Nothing will be left but microparticles when I'm done with him."

Yvonne objected quietly.

„But first you have to know who it is."

MM glared at his wife.

„That's just a matter of time. The task that I can not master has yet to be invented."

„Let's have a coffee first, MM. We have to think about what to do."

„You are welcome to make a coffee. But you better leave that stupid guy to me. After all, it's my money alone that he has stolen."

When the coffee, which he had taken without another comment, was emptied, he announced.

„We'll go into his game, apparently. This will give us valuable time. Now it's time to go to bed. Tomorrow we must be rested. Did you already check in which city the given coordinates are located?"

„Gonne do it in a bit, MM."

At the beginning of her relationship, she had been annoyed that on one hand MM did not trust her to think about a problem in a rational way, but on the other hand was dependent on her as soon as it was about research on the Internet. In the meantime, she found that only amusing. She googled the coordinates and had the result already on the screen.

„Cologne. To be precise, it is the Roman Germanic Museum." she called over her shoulder into the house.

„Cologne" he grimaced in disgust. „There's always this awful Christopher Street Day happening. I hope no gays grapple on me."

„Don't you think that you are exaggerating something? First, Cologne is not just gay. And second, gays do not grab any men just because they're gay. After all, you are not constantly tackled by heterosexual women, do you?"

„Do you make yourself strong for minorities or what is going on here?"

„I'm just trying to make you understand that you have a rather heavy and illogical prejudice about gay people."

„This is not a prejudice."

„What else?"

Yvonne's eyes showed honest interest in his answer. He made a dismissive gesture and pushed off towards the bathroom.

„You do not understand anything."

After a short night they were already at 11 o'clock on the Roncalliplatz right in front of the museum. Already on the drive they had puzzled how the contact to the thief would take place. He had probably chosen a public place so he would have a better chance of disappearing back into the crowd. They saw the big shopping street, where the tourists crowded close. Ideal conditions to disappear in the crowd. To bridge the time, they went briefly to the cathedral, which stands right next to the museum.

When they wanted to enter the museum at 12 o'clock, somebody tapped MMs shoulder.

„You're MM and Yvonne?"

In front of them stood one of the young skateboarders who presented their tricks on the square.

„That's us."

MM looked attentively at the young man.

„This is for you."

He handed MM an envelope and drove back to his buddies without any particular hurry.

„Hey wait. Who gave you the letter? What did he look like?"

The skateboarder made an elegant turnaround and stood in front of MM with a slightly annoyed expression.

„I thought of something like that. As if that would be a simple job. Listen. Such a guy with sunglasses, trench coat chatted me up. He looked as if he had just stepped out of some stupid agent movie. Striking unremarkable. He told me something about a chase among friends and gave me your photograph."

He pulled a crumpled photo from his pocket and handed it to MM.

„Told me I only had to wait until 12 and was gone."

„How much money did he give you?"

„That does not concern you. May I recommend myself?"

He made a formal bow and was gone. This time he did not react to the call of MM.

„What is in the letter?" Yvonne wanted to know. MM opened the letter and read it aloud.

„*I congratulate. You have decided to play with me. Have a nice day in Cologne. The next clue you'll find tomorrow in your mail.*"

MM stared at the letter for a long time. Finally he started laughing.

„This can only be a joke. You will see, when we are at home, some of my friends will show up and have a great time enjoying the successful joke. And I fell for it."

„Who could that be?" Yvonne thought aloud. „Of course we do not have real best friends."

MM gave her a quick look and then hugged her in a good mood.

„The best we go first in one of the taverns and eat something of the local food. They should cook here especially good chicken."

A little later, his mood had returned to a low point.

„Never in my life has anyone thrown me out of a guest house."

„You should have read the menu better before you ordered the Halver Hahn" Yvonne objected.

„This funny waiter was just waiting for some tourist to fall into the trap. I have only exercised my right to complain about this behavior."

Yvonne smiled at him.

„And he did not like that, my dear MM."

He looked at her lovingly.

„You really are the only one who can say that to me. Alright, I'm ready to let that go."

They stayed in town for a few more hours and were not home until late in the evening.

[Note from the author: 'Halver Hahn' is a rye roll with cheese. The look is reminiscent of a fried half chicken. Even german-speaking tourists translate the typical Cologne term with 'fried half chicken'

In a typical Cologne brewery, it is part of the waiter's right to rebuke the guests if they do not behave.]

Monday 2nd May

„Mr. Müller, there is a consignment that is addressed to you. Personally."

„If it is that what you're saying, do not make a long speech. Just put it on my desktop" MM snapped at his secretary. „I'll see it soon enough."

The secretary seemed to be accustomed to this treatment, as she answered him with no apparent emotion.

„I would have done that if the envelope did not show any other abnormalities. There is a photo of you and your wife printed, showing you in front of a background unknown to me. Apparently a photomontage."

„What are you talking about? I did not order any envelopes with such photos. Give it to me!"

She handed him the envelope and disappeared quickly from his office.

One look was enough to tell him that the photo was taken during her visit to Cologne. It showed him and Yvonne when the skateboarder handed him the letter. The background, however, was replaced by a large poster advertising Christopher Street Day. When he opened the envelope, he found a short note and a CD.

„This is the second game and therefore your second city trip. There is a little game on the CD. It has a very simple interface. I hope you are not disappointed. In the game you have to find some solutions that I would classify in the area of general knowledge. So please do not be offended if you feel under-challenged. As soon as all tasks have been solved, an indication of the next city appears. I would like to ask you to follow this advice."

„Mrs Schütich, I'm not coming in again today. If something is urgent, send me a text message."

Before the secretary could reply, he was already through the door. She picked up the phone

„He will not come in again today. You won the bet."

She listened to the phone.

„Yes, I could have imagined it. No matter. Are we going to meet tonight? I'll cook. Betting debts are honorary debts."

The rest of the working day was, as always, when the boss was not in the house, very relaxed and therefore very effective.

Already from the car MM called the detective agency Triebel.

„MM speaking. I need you in 30 minutes. At my home address."

He ended the call before he could be given an answer. When he arrived at his house, he called Yvonne.

„The blackmailer has contacted again. Here is a CD with a game. Look into that and tell me the solution right away. I have no time for such nonsense. Triebel will be here straight away."

„Nice that you are already at home dearest MM. I am also happy to see you."

The tone was accusation enough. MM looked at his wife in surprise, but did not respond. Other things were more important to him.

„Imagine, the blackmailer sent a mail to the office. This is the envelope."

He held out the photo.

„He watched us at the handover. We could have come up with that as well."

„Did you see what's on the poster in the background? I do not want to know who else has seen the envelope except the Schütich. Outrageous. He wants to make me a non-person in my own company."

Before Yvonne could reply, the doorbell rang.

„That will be Triebel. Once you have solved the game, you join us and tell us the solution."

Yvonne was left with a raised eyebrow. At the moment she seemed to be nothing more than a useful office worker for MM.

Such thoughts did not come to MMs mind. He opened the door for Triebel, immediately led him into his office and gave a strictly chronological account of what had happened so far.

Meanwhile, with the help of the Internet, Yvonne began to work through the questions asked by the program on the CD.

When MM told the Cologne-story, Triebel could not hold back anymore.

„The trip to Cologne could have been the end of the blackmail. It was crystal clear that the blackmailer would be there on the first rendezvous to see if you would turn up."

It took MM a moment to swallow his anger. He wasn't used to be interrupted. And not at all, he was just to be reprimanded, though he had to admitted his mistake reluctantly.

„I'm sure that there will be a second date. When will that be? Did the blackmailer contact again since yesterday?"

MM pointed to the envelope.

„It was in the office-mail today."

Triebel put on gloves and took the enclosed note from the envelope. After reading it, he asked for the CD.

„I gave that to my wife. She is currently in the process of solving the game announced here."

The detective looked at him dumbfounded.

„MM, you do not want to tell me now that you simply went to your computer with this CD?"

„What should happen? Do you think the computer evaporates into thin air or something?"

MM wanted to know with a superior smile. Triebel managed to stay calm.

„Ever heard of viruses, trojans and all the other stuff that can infect a computer these days? You can't just put the CD of a stranger, even a blackmailer, just like that in your computer. Where do I find the computer?"

When they joined Yvonne, she looked at the printer in amazement.

„Is anything special happening Yvonne?"

She looked at MM.

„Not 'til right now. I have just answered the last question. No idea why the printer is printing now."

All three looked at the freshly printed sheet.

„It is not known whether he had met one, but if he did, then he could have said: Whom did he meet here? Anna? And with a slight smile on his lips he would certainly have given the word 'here' a special emphasis. One could have thought that the word would have merged with the subsequent word."

On the screen appeared „mission accomplished".

„What does that mean?" MM looked questioningly at Yvonne.

„That's what Bush said back then, when he thought his soldiers had conquered Iraq" Yvonne told him.

„Of course, I know that. I want to know what that means here on my screen."

At the very moment the screen went black.

MM pressed the keyboard, moved the mouse, but nothing happened. Finally he switched off the computer via the main switch and started it again immediately. After a short time, the computer reported countless errors and the recommendation to call an old system recovery file.

Triebel sighed.

„I just told you. The CD was certainly programmed with a powerful virus that has now demolished your computer. Let an expert work on it. Maybe he can save something. Were important data on the computer?"

MM shook his head.

„No, this computer is actually more for gaming and the internet. I'll quickly replace it."

„At least now we know what he meant by 'mission accomplished'" Yvonne interjected. „Probably that was the moment he knew the computer was junk."

„Thank you very much, Yvonne, I would have never thought of that." MM answered in a bad mood.

Back in MMs office, Triebel wondered what the meaning of the printed message was. MM nodded.

„Definitely the next city. Wondering only where that can be hidden in this message."

„I think that's not hard." Yvonne said optimistically. „All the other puzzles from the game were very easy to solve with the internet. Actually, even partially without internet."

Both men looked at her expectantly.

„I would simply enter 'hieranna' as the search term and then see what happens. After all, he attached great importance to pronouncing the two words as one single word."

[Note from the author: English 'here' = German 'hier']

„Okay, take the laptop and see what you find out" MM asked her.

As she was starting the laptop, the doorbell rang.

„Express delivery for Mr. Müller."

MM accepted the letter. Before he could open it, Triebel took the letter out of his hand.

„You do not want to blur again possible traces?"

MM reached out to reclaim the letter.

„I am allowed to open my mail in my house! You should rather take care of this blackmailer!"

Triebel looked challengingly at MM.

„When was the last time you received an express delivery with business documents home?"

„Never, but sometime is always the first time."

„With all respect MM. You're making it really easy for your blackmailer. Take a look at the sender. This is the same as that of the letter with the CD."

MM stepped back from Triebel.

„For years, I have spared no sacrifices to bring my company forward. Since it is quite normal that I first think of the company, if I get an express delivery."

Yvonne came into the room with the laptop open.

„Erfurt."

She looked triumphantly at the two men.

„I would say it's Erfurt. When googling 'hieranna' it is corrected to 'Hirana'. This is the name of the Erfurt University in the times of Luther."

Actually, she had expected more joy about the quick fix of the puzzle. Finally, her eyes fell on the express letter.

„What's that?"

„Another letter. So, I think another letter from the blackmailer."

With a relativizing gesture, MM added.

„Looks like this."

Meanwhile Triebel had opened his small emergency case and pulled out a scalpel, with which he carefully opened the letter. Using tweezers, he pulled out the writing and held it so that MM could read.

„MM, you're a man of action, a true doer, as you'll never get tired of pointing out. Now, presumably a computer will have landed in the realm of eternal hunting grounds. I sincerely hope that the print was clear enough for you, because the exact address in the city is too general to find the city without further help. Tomorrow morning (Tuesday) 11am Hauptstraße 5. The codeword is 'Dali'. I expect punctual appearance.

If you do not show up, I'll think about how I can motivate you better in the future. An exit from the whole issue is not provided by my side. If you want to get out, then this is only possible by a self-report and of course the renunciation of the money.

Another private word: Of course, I understand if you try to track me down. If this succeeds, I will prove to be a fair loser. However, I assume that you will not ask other people for help."

Triebel was the first to break the silence.

„He's crazy. But that's exactly our chance. I will assign a friendly agency in Erfurt with the observation of the address."

He waited for MMs consent and then took his cell phone.

„Hello Mike, this is Triebel. Can you help me out tomorrow morning?"

He signaled success with his thumbs up.

„The address is Erfurt, Hauptstraße 5. My clients are there for 11am tomorrow morning. Discretion is the top priority. You probably will not be the only one who will observe. I want to know who the other person is. I'll send the photos of my clients right away."

After hanging up, he turned back to MM.

„MM, please give me a list of what was in the safe. Maybe it can conclude a trace."

„The list is done quickly: Money, nothing but money."

„Sorry, but what does he mean by self-report?"

„How should I know that?"

„MM, since your wife is currently out of the room, I ask the obvious question. We both did a lot of questionable things. Were any incriminating documents in the safe? Or are you storing those things in a different location?"

„No"

„What do you mean by 'no'?"

„No, I don't store them at any other place."

MM was annoyed.

„You tell me that the blackmailer now has tons of incriminating material in his hands?" Triebel clearly had trouble staying calm. „Why do I get that information only after repeated request? Do you even have a clue what the blackmailer can do to both of us?"

„Well, it's not that bad. Finally, he must also be able to properly evaluate the documents" MM tried to calm him down.

„When did you intend to tell me that?"

When MM did not answer, Triebel continued.

„Doesn't matter. Assume that he can do something with the things. That would also explain that he is writing such strange mails. I'm sure if we want to find him, we have to look for our old 'clients'."

„But they all were idiots. None of those can break in and then crack the safe. Do not be ridiculous. This must be a very

26

well-done professional burglar. And for him the documents are just worthless bycatch."

Triebel looked at MM for a long time.

„Do you actually believe what you are saying? Just because we pulled a fast one on those guys, they are not just the pure losers. While you are in Erfurt tomorrow, I will scour the old documents and sort out who we need to take a closer look at."

MM made a dismissive gesture.

„I can not stop you. But tomorrow we'll know who it is anyway, provided that your friends in Erfurt understand their job."

„I would like to have your sunny spirit. In which code of law is written that the blackmailer has to be in Erfurt tomorrow? The observation can be a success and just as well a failure. And this is completely independent of the abilities of my colleagues."

„Show me the lock, please" Triebel continued after a short break. MM looked at him questioningly.

„Which lock?"

„Yesterday your lock was glued. I want to take a look at it."

„Of course, that's in the trash where it belongs. In the meantime, it has been replaced and everything is in perfect order again."

Again, Triebel gave MM a long look.

„Ever heard of forensics? How did the guy get in? Any traces? Battered windows or similar?"

„Nothing. That must have been a professional. Presumably he broke the lock and then, to cover the tracks, he made this glue thing!"

„Do you mind if I look at your house more closely?"

MM made a welcoming gesture.

„Feel free to do what you want to do."

Tuesday 3rd May

11 o'clock, Erfurt. The two were standing in front of a nail salon.

„What should that be now?"

„No idea MM. Let's just go and ask if the keyword 'Dali' says something to them" Yvonne suggested as she already pushed the door open. MM followed her hesitantly.

Immediately she met a young employee. His name tag told her that it was Detlef.

„Good day, what can I do for you?"

„Hello Detlef. I'm Yvonne. What does ‚Dali' tell you?"

„Easy. That was a great artist of surrealism."

Seeing the disappointed faces of Yvonne and MM, he added: „Just kidding. There is a kind of blind date at 11 o'clock. Keyword 'Dali'. You make a kind of surprise game for adults?"

„Yes, something like that" Yvonne agreed with relief. „And what do we win here?"

„Well, wonderful long nails for you, of course." With a re-gretful look to MM, he added „Unfortunately nothing for you. Unless you want the nails? In that case I agree to throw a coin or pay the second treatment out of my own pocket."

When he saw MMs face, he quickly added, „kidding".

Before MM could answer, Yvonne advised him to spend the next hour in one of the cafes.

„I'll call you on the phone when I'm done."

„I would expect two to three hours" interjected Detlef. Without a word MM left the nail salon and walked off towards the city center. Detlef looked after him.

„Well, he is disappointed that he won nothing, right?"

„I do not think so." Yvonne told him. „He is just annoyed that this will take so long."

„If I could perform miracles, I would first conjure up a lot of money. But I am not a magician. So I have to earn my money normally. And that's why I have the great pleasure to do your nails"

He looked at Yvonne.

„You will not quit your thrilling game?"

„No not at all. Although I consider the idea to be a bit extravagant., I'm looking forward to this event with some excitement. I assume that I have no say?"

„Yes" Detlef agreed. „Everything is already set and paid for."

He led Yvonne to one of the treatment tables.

„Shall we?"

„Get started, Detlef."

Three hours later she had new nails that were anything but a discreet French design with a few patterns. All nails extended an centimeter beyond the fingertips. On each thumb was a giraffe whose legs were so oversized that they could have come from a Dali painting. The remaining fingernails had received no pictures. They were shiny silver. Even more like chrome.

After Yvonne had looked thoughtfully at the fingers for a while, Detlef explained to her that she did not have to worry about losing one of her nails. They would withstand every mechanical stress. „And the length is not a problem. You will quickly get used to it. There are women who are getting along with much longer nails for years."

Yvonne was not so sure but did not want to discuss that matter. First, she had to try out how she could cope with her new nails. As she said goodbye to the nail designer, he gave her a small envelope.

„That's for your husband. Probably the next station that your friend comes up with. I'm sure your husband will have lots of fun."

Arriving at the street, Yvonne had some trouble digging her cell phone out of her pocket.

„MM? I'm done here. Where can I find you?" She walked along the parked cars. One had the back window slightly open. Probably a dog sat behind the tinted glass and waited patiently for the return of his master. „How my nails look

29

alike? I would say indescribable." She chuckled into the phone. „See you soon."

A little later she saw MM approaching at the end of the street. For the surprise to be perfect, she put her hands in her coat pockets.

„Yvonne, let me see!"

With a big fuss she took her hands out of the pockets and looked into the disbelieving face of MM.

„Take a pair of scissors and cut them off immediately. That looks disgusting. Or better, you go back to that guy right away and let him remove it!"

„Do not get so upset. Before I do anything I would recommend reading this letter first." She handed him the envelope. „That's what Detlef gave me."

„Who is Detlef?"

His face seemed to turn red in the very next moment.

„The nail designer, whom I have to thank for these wonderful nails."

„Now please do not tell me that you like them!"

Yvonne looked at the nails again

„Yes, they are something. Not the boring French design that everyone has."

„The what?"

„You know it. The tips are white and the rest more or less in its natural color."

„That's what it's called?" nodded MM while he took the letter with a sullen look. „He could have given me that directly too."

„He would not MM. He is of the opinion that this is just a game for rich people who know nothing else to do with their time. He won't infringe instructions he has been given."

While MM was already reading the letter, he only half-heartedly agreed with her. An instant later he stared at her dumbfounded.

„What's up? What does it say?"

As he didn't answer she took the paper out of his hand and read it herself.

„Since Yvonne now has such wonderful nails, you, dear MM, should not get the feeling of being neglected. You are expected at 3pm in the Rathausstraße 15. Of course, I know that you can not handle surprises so well. That's why I'll tell you now that you have an appointment for a warm wax depilation of all your body hair. Of course, only the part that is below the neck. I appreciate your willingness to suffer a little bit for me.

I'll get back to you in the next few days.

PS.: Yvonne, please keep your nails as they are. It's better for everyone involved."

Yvonne could not help but chuckle, which gave her an aggressive glance from MM.

„Do you think that's funny? Am I surrounded by no one else but idiots? I'll never do that. He can do that by himself. How could I be so stupid to get my hair ripped?"

„Because the blackmailer wants that?"

„Cause the blackmailer wants that." He aped Yvonne. „That's no reason for me!"

„Your problem MM. At least if the blackmailer makes a problem out of it. But then it is your problem and not mine. At least I hope the blackmailer sees it that way too."

MM looked at her confused.

„Are you serious now? Where should the little wretch cause me a problem? He is now under surveillance and will be delivered on a golden tray."

„If that's what you mean."

After an hour on the highway, they stopped at a rest area to fill their tummy for the rest of their return journey. As they were sitting, MMs phone rang.

„Who is it Triebel?"

As MM listened to the answer, Yvonne could tell by his face color that the answer was not to MMs liking.

„Do you want to fool me or what should that be?"

MM did not bother to lower his voice, which gave him the full attention of the next tables

„You are working with suckers! Worthless, stupid suckers! He should not bother to send a bill!"

He allowed Triebel to speak for only a few seconds before he interrupted again

„I expect you at 8pm at my home. The conversation is over!"

MM pressed with all his strength on the button with which he broke the connection.

Yvonne had sat relaxed in her chair during the conversation.

„Oh, what were those good times, when you could slam the phone on the cradle."

She earned an aggressive look from MM.

„What is that supposed to tell me?"

„Well, just as you have pressed the touch screen button, it is logical to assume that you would rather have had a real phone with the real phone cradle."

He looked at her for a long time, while his facial features slowly relaxing.

„How can you always stay so calm?"

„It does not help when I get upset. Simple as it is."

„Simple. Super. I do not think that's easy. If I must have an outlet, I can not begin to tell myself a story about relaxing and staying calm."

Yvonne noticed that the people around her turned back to their own conversations.

„What did Triebel tell you?"

„The employee of his friend. The one who should take the photos. He has been stolen the car. Everything is gone."

„What's 'everything' in this case?"

„What do you think, what I mean by 'everything'? The photos, the equipment, everything! The idiot was around the corner for peeing. When he came back, the car was gone."

„Well, then waxing would have been the better choice?"

„He'll never get me there. I'm not a chick!"

„But still worth to be considered. Your back looks pretty monkey-like."

MM stared at her in sudden understanding.

„You are in cahoots with him? You're annoying me with your hair removal remarks since several month. Is this your way to get me into that?"

„Sure and by the way, I also steal a car that I do not know what it is. I have to consider myself as real heroine."

She could see, that he was fighting with his anger. Finally, to her astonishment, he was able to mutter: „Then you just do not stick together with him."

Yvonne smiled at him.

„If this is something like an apology, then I'll accept it."

As always with such things, MM did not seem to understand what she meant.

„It was a natural approach. That's all."

In the evening they were already expected by Triebel.

„My colleague has equipped the car with a tracking system. The thief parked it in front of the police-station in the absolute ban. They have towed it away. He just ransomed it. Of course, all valuables are gone."

MM banged his fist on the table.

„With what fools are you working together? Get the car stolen. Did he at least store in his useless brain any pictures that would take us further?"

„No abnormalities."

„You want to tell me that we are still at the very beginning?"

Triebel barely withstood his gaze.

„Unfortunately, that's the way it is."

„Then I hope that you now have a reasonable plan B in your pocket. Otherwise, I'm looking for a more capable detective!"

„We can come clear with the police in Erfurt. They can certainly detect DNA traces. Then he is trapped."

„You can't be serious. I can't understand how you're even able to get such an idea. Then I can tell them immediately, why the man was observing."

„We just have to come up with a story" Triebel suggested.

MM wiped of the proposal with a single wave of his hand.

„Forget it. The cops hear every day stories like that. Anyone who thinks he could exploit them for his own purposes has almost lost."

When Triebel was silent, MM got up.

„We stop it for today. Tomorrow I expect a brilliant idea. Goodbye."

Wednesday 4th May

„Hello MM. The postman was just here. I want to bet that this very letter is from the blackmailer. Should I open it?"

She could hear through the telephone line how a heavy object crashed. Then the office door opened. Surely Ms. Schütich had just come to his office to check on what is happening. Yvonne heard him instruct his secretary to deal with the shards later. Then he told Yvonne that he would be home in a few minutes.

Yvonne looked at her nails. She had searched the pictures in an art book about Dali. Without success. Nevertheless, she was confirmed that they could have been designed by Dali. They conveyed the feeling of being small human beings that depend on the mercy of gigantic monsters.

A little later, the front door was torn open and MM rushed into the house.

„Where is the letter?"

In tow Triebel also came into the room. He had already drawn his scalpel and started opening the envelope. There were two photos in the envelope. One showed a kind of victory column and the other a palace somewhere in a city center. And, of course, they found again a message.

„First, let me briefly review your visit to Erfurt. Yvonne, you behaved brilliantly. My congratulations.

MM, you really worry me. It was all arranged and you little coward are drawing in your horns. That did not please me. I have been very clear that you're not allowed to get assist from any detective. But you thought, you could hire an amateur to take pictures. Did you really believe, I parade up and down to pose? When he had to pee - you should point out to him once that peeing in public is a misdemeanor - I parked the car. Let's forget it. Was a refreshing little fun. I should really thank you for that.

Now the next task. Incidentally, I recommend staying in this city that you will visit for a while. It's worth it. But one thing after the other.

Find a city where you can copy the photos attached to this letter. Please make sure that your clothing is modeled on the original in the photo.

Dear Yvonne, since you behaved well in Erfurt, it is okay for me, if you pose in a proper dress with the wreath in front of the pillar. You can do without the color.

Dear MM, since you've been messing around in Erfurt, you can play the role of the person in black, that can be admired in the other photo. It would be nice if your head is clearly visible.

If you had the kindness to send me the digital results the day after tomorrow? Evening would be okay.

Have fun shopping and of course doing some nice pictures.

As a last reminder, I would not fail to add that I do not want you to get help from others to find me or otherwise escape the situation. Would be really good if you finally understood that, MM."

MM stared at the picture in disbelief. The person he had to play was dressed in black, wore boots with block heels, a pair of tight, shiny trousers, a short sticking out skirt, a shiny top and a thick leather collar with a large ring in front.

„He does not really believe that?" He threw the photo on the table and glanced at Yvonne and Triebel. „No way am I going with such nonsense. When and how do you finally catch him, Triebel?"

„We have to go into lengthy research. Your next action has to be planned carefully. There is a lot of work ahead of us."

„What do you mean with 'Your next action'? Do you think that I am part of the shit or what? I truly have better things to do than that."

Triebel tried to make him listen with a mollifying gesture.

36

„We're running out of time. For me, it looks like the black-mailer has a considerable lead. We have to catch up first. We need time for that. He knows that, because he keeps up the pace and hopes that we will continue to react, not to act. Therefore, it is important to join all forces. And that is, what we need time for. And the easiest way to gain time is to go into your next challenge. But if you do not, then he certainly has the option to act stricter. That would make it even harder for us to pick up a trace."

Triebel made a pause for effect.

„The question we can't answer is: How far is he willing to go and how much fun does he want to have with the whole story? In other words: When will he give the documents to the authorities and end the whole game?"

MM couldn't believe his ears.

„Did you just say 'game'? That's not a game!"

„The blackmailer calls it that, so it's the way we have to see it. To a certain extent, one must adopt the opponents' thoughts. The very fact that he calls it a game means that he will not finish the whole thing quickly. Nevertheless, we should not provoke him without a reasonable plan."

„So, what do you suggest?" In MMs voice was a slight sign of frustration.

„What I just said. Join the next challenge and at the same time scour our old cases. I am sure that we will find an approach there."

To give the signal for the end of the meeting, MM hit the thighs.

„We'll stop the blackmailer by pretending to be on it. That means we're going to that city to make him believe we're in it, but we certainly do not do the photos, at least mine. He gets a photomontage."

„In the first letter, however, the blackmailer warned us to cheat him. You're not worried that he will find out?" Yvonne suggested.

MM made a dismissive gesture.

„If you really want to take your picture, then we'll do it. After all, that's your poor limit. Always be beautiful and always be good. That's all you can do. But this man does not get me into such clothes. The photo in front of the castle takes place without me."

Thoughtfully, he touched his chin.

„We'll do it this way: You get these awful clothes. We take a photo here in the garden and then you put it in the picture of the castle. You can do that, right?"

Yvonne nodded. „Yes, but if he's a pro, he'll notice. That's inevitable."

„Yvonne, you are gigantic. He'll be too happy to see me in those disgusting clothes in front of the castle. He will never check whether the photo is real."

He gave her a hug.

„And you Triebel, go to the city and catch the guy, if he gads around there. This time do not ask any buddies. Clear?"

Yvonne took the pictures and disappeared towards the computer to google the solution.

„MM?" Triebel had drawn a notepad and a ball pen. „You didn't do recent acquisitions I don't know about?"

After a moment's reflection, MM named four names.

„All bunglers who did not understand their business. It is actually quite simple. Place an order that is too big for the company and be merciless when it comes to deadlines. That's it."

He briefly outlined the individual cases until Yvonne returned.

„It was pretty easy again." She pointed to the first photo. „This is the Luxembourg flag. So, I searched for sights in Luxembourg. You see the board on the pillar? It says 'gelle fra'. Easy to find." Yvonne looked at the two men. „That means 'Golden Woman'. The second photo shows the Palace of the Grand Dukes. That's in Luxembourg downtown."

She leaned back satisfied and smiling.

„So, we'll be in Luxembourg the day after tomorrow. And then it's over" stated MM, looking past Yvonne on Triebel.

Thursday 5th May

„Yvonne, will you please hand me another roll?"

She held out the small breadbasket.

„What else was in the vault MM?"

He looked at her for a while.

„How do you know that there was more inside? One million cash is enough, isn't it? Why do you even ask that? You heard what I talked about with Triebel. It was yesterday. You remember?"

Yvonne nodded in agreement.

„Sure, but I think that you talked to him a few other things when I was not in the room."

MM smiled at her.

„So at least you can use your own head sometimes. Okay, there was more in it. Papers that should not fall into the wrong hands." He added with a straight face. „When he realizes the importance of the documents, he has me on toast."

„What do you mean exactly?"

„Some documents just have to be kept outside the shop. If a person is as successful as I am, then sometimes that person has to go new ways. Nothing for cowards."

Yvonne did not want to hear a long talk from and about her 'brilliant' husband. So she stopped it directly.

„I'm off to get my outfit for the photos. I assume that you would like to buy yours by your own?"

Just before he blushed, he noticed her innocent smile and disappeared towards the company. A tough day is breaking for your employees again, she thought as she saw him driving off the driveway.

★★★

Triebel had already been viewing the old documents for the entire morning. In each case, they had followed the same pattern. Monitor the victim's environment as far as possible. Business relations, family situation, loyalty to the spouse etc. Most of the time they had found something to start with. Now the same material had to be useful to find a clue to the black-mailer. After some time, he had made a closer circle of three victims, whom he would trust the blackmail. He spent the rest of the day updating the data for all three of them. In the age of the Internet, this work was much easier than it was years ago, when they had to rummage innumerable address books. They used to have some special friends that offered illegal ser-vices. Now such help was needed only at a much later stage of investigation.

In the evening, the files were sufficient refreshed. Now Triebel was able to get a clear picture.

***

Yvonne started the shopping tour looking for her dress. The saleswoman was thrilled with the idea of recreating the 'gelle fra'. With the help of the photo they found the right dress after a short time. In one of the many other shops Yvonne bought the laurel wreath and was done with it.

With some uncertainty, she went to an adult shop to buy the pieces for MM. To her delight, the saleswoman seemed to be at least as helpful as the saleswoman at the dress. She just had to show the photo.

„That's what I need for my husband. Can you help me with that?"

The woman glanced at the photo.

„Wow. Where did you get that?"

Yvonne looked at the saleswoman at a loss.

„Well, the nails! Are they chrome plated?"

„No, that's some kind of special paint and a lot of polish-ing."

„Every morning?"

‚Why not?' Yvonne thought. „Yes, of course, every morn-ing. Otherwise they become dull."

Her eyes took the name tag of the young woman.

„May I call you Beatrice?"

„Of course."

„Okay Beatrice, what do you think about the photo? I need the complete outfit."

Beatrice took the picture.

„I can not tell exactly if it's PVC or latex. However, since you do not have your husband with you, I would definitely recommend latex. This is much more elastic. To be honest, I always recommend latex. Especially with the initial equipment. That's an initial equipment, right?"

Yvonne nodded in agreement and called MMs sizes. Beatrice pulled a legging and a short-sleeved shirt off the shelf with a steady hand.

„Then you need the boots. Since we have exactly the right model with 10cm heel. Actually, all beginners are doing well with those boots. The shafts are also made of latex. Your husband will love them."

She pulled a strap from the adjacent shelf.

„You want to lock the boots?"

Yvonne could not help laughing. MM would anyway make an act out of the little photo-shoot. A lock on his boots would probably mean the end of it.

„No, I better not. I do not want to overextend him."

She looked around the shop, searching.

„Then only the collar would be missing."

Beatrice went purposefully to the appropriate shelf.

„Lockable or not lockable?"

Yvonne could not resist a second time. She took it with a lock. Since it did not necessarily have to be locked it was just an option. Maybe the blackmailer had something in mind anyway. Then she would have done at least this purchase already. As long as MM refused to follow his instructions, she did not know what the blackmailer had in mind.

Beatrice looked at her expectantly.

„Can I do anything else for you?"

„No thanks Beatrice. Let's see, maybe I'll be back soon."

Beatrice looked again at the picture.

„We almost forgot the absolute highlight. The skirt."

„Right" Yvonne agreed. „Do you have something like that?"

Beatrice pulled a pack from the shelf.

„I would recommend such a pleated skirt. It is, however made of slightly stiffer PVC. You do not get that 'sticking out' - effect with latex. Or you do it with one or two petticoats. Only those can be seen and would create a different overall view."

That sounded convincing to Yvonne.

„Okay, so I really have everything now?"

After a scrutinizing look at the photo, the two went to checkout.

„I'm sure, you will have lots of fun. Would be glad if I could welcome you soon again."

„It depends on this evening."

„Wait" Beatrice handed her a small spray bottle. „Shine-Spray. This will make him shine. As the name indicates."

Yvonne left the store knowing that shopping at the adult store was also fun.

„Yvonne, I can not make it for dinner. I've gotten an urgent meeting in between."

„What about the photo MM? I thought we would do it to-day. But we need daylight for that."

After a few heavy breaths, he informed Yvonne that there would be time for it the next day after the stupid trip to Lux-embourg. Then he ended the conversation.

Yvonne's eyes went to the shopping she had draped on the sofa. Beatrice had even packed a catalog and her business card. Why not? Sure, the clothes would fit her much better than MM. Finally, she also had the much cooler fingernails. Overall, MM was stronger than she was, but there was little difference in body size.

A little later she stood in black in front of the big mirror in the bedroom. She had to concede to the blackmailer that the combination had a certain aura. The feeling of looking at her-self in the mirror while she ran her long fingernails over her body was almost indescribable. But before she forgot herself, she forced herself to take off her clothes. When she wanted to open the necklace, she remembered to her horror that she had seen no key in the package. She searched frantically everything, but was unsuccessful. She could not possibly wait with the collar around her neck until MM came back and ask him to get it off somehow. He would probably first disengage again and then - as so often in manual skills - prove to be absolute loser. Beatrice' business card caught her eyes.

„No problem. Just come over" was her redeeming answer.

Later in the shop Beatrice could not help laughing as Yvonne stood in front of her despite the summery temperatures with a turtleneck.

„You just have to wear the collar as if those who have no collar are among the outsiders of society" Beatrice explained to her.

„Talk is cheap. After all, you do not run around with a collar, whose key is nowhere to be found." countered Yvonne.

„No, but with locks around my boots. And the keys are at my friend's home. This is not quite as conspicuous, but brings me some looks outside of this store."

She lifted one of her feet as proof. Yvonne had not noticed the boots before.

„Wow. Real high heels."

„They just look tall. It's due to the stiletto heels. I'm used to that by now. Nevertheless, you will notice your feet when you have to spend half the day in such stilettos. But my friend and I enjoy this little game. So, it's okay."

Yvonne kept looking at the heels.

„Why didn't I notice that this morning?"

„Don't worry about that." Beatrice smiled. „At some customers, I'm pretty much sure that they go to a store like this for the first time. They always try to act relaxed but in reality, they are so excited that they can hardly think clearly. You are also part of it."

„I really appeared so excited?" After a short break, she added. „By the way, I'm Yvonne. In the rescue action that we still have in front of us, I believe this is more appropriate."

„With pleasure. I'm Beatrice, but you already know that." She pointed to a stool beside her. „Then sit down. I'll just get the emergency key bundle."

When she came back, she had a huge bunch of keys that would have been fine with any jailer.

„Luckily you bought a reasonably priced entry-level model. There are always cheap locks on it. I am sure that I do not have to search for the right key for a long time."

In fact, the tenth attempt was crowned with success.

„Now you have to tell me how it happened. I thought you wanted to dress your husband, not the other way around."

Yvonne made a dismissive gesture.

„He will get home today much later than announced. And when I saw those things lying there, I thought to myself that I could actually try them on."

Beatrice looked surprised

„And?"

„I put it on and then got the problem with the collar. You know the rest of the story."

„So lucky that it did not happen to you with the boots."

„Why?"

„Because your sweater is not long enough to cover up."

„There would have been an even bigger problem" Yvonne laughed. „They are a few sizes too large for me. That was not what I would define as a safe walk."

„Do you want to put on the right size?"

Yvonne did not have to think twice. Since she was now free of the collar, she had nothing important to do in the next few hours.

„Why not?"

In the end, Yvonne left the store with a pair of overknees who had a twelve-centimeter stiletto heel and a small plateau. She had planned to practice at home every morning. The stunning view at her legs in those boots had been breathtaking.

***

It was remarkably easy to get into the small family home. The front door was neatly closed, but the cellar door was simply pulled shut and had a cheap lock. Very careless. Since he was once in the basement, he began there with the search. He was not sure what he was looking for, but that was the interesting thing about it.

As always, he divided his visit into two parts. First, it was about a rough overview. Here and there lift something, nothing more. After a quarter of an hour he had once worked through the whole house. The most attractive room was undoubtedly the study, which was directly adjacent to the living room. From here he was able to keep a good eye on the entrance area. At the same time, he was protected from prying eyes out of the neighborhood.

The negligence of the homeowner continued in the study without interruption. Did people no longer have any sense of wrongdoing? Such sensible documents could not be kept so easily accessible by a reasonable person. He had taken extra time to search everything without stressing himself before the homeowner would return, and now realized that he had finished in between less than an hour later. He selected the most interesting files and put them in his briefcase. Now he had several hours of idle. Just because all the files were kept so easily accessible.

Finally, after far too long, the front door opened. He spoke as the person entered the living room.

„Good evening, Mr. Triebel."

The person addressed turned to the unexpected guest.

„How did you come to my house?"

„Respect. Most of the others would not have said anything at first or tried to flee the house." He made an elegant bow. „Chapeau!"

Triebel unobtrusively tried to fetch the cell phone from his jacket pocket.

„What do you want? Where should this lead?

„I am happy to answer this question but would like to ask you to keep your hands steady."

As Triebel paused in his movement, he continued.

„I do not really want much. You should just make my acquaintance. I am the one you are looking for on behalf of a certain MM. Or to be precise, I am actually just the executive organ of the actual client. Although this description actually does not really apply, as I am more likely to be described as the dark side of the client. In something like a metaphysical sense. It's not easy to describe that precisely. Will you do me a favor and sit down somewhere? I would like to have an intensive conversation about it. If you would like that too."

Triebel moved slowly in the direction of the man.

„I do not understand the messy stuff you're talking about. I urge you to leave my house."

To confirm, he pointed to the front door.

„Well, then I will do that. I do not consider myself to be unpolite. Your house, your rules. I just wanted to explain who I am and what you're dealing with."

Triebel had expected everything. But not this answer. In the final analysis this didn't matter at all because there was a second perception that he did not understand fast enough. His uninvited guest suddenly held a weapon in his hand. Triebel could see the typical extension. A silencer. He had no time to think about it, since he was already dead when he hit the ground.

„Messy stuff. What do you imagine? You were clearly not in the position to irritate your opponent recklessly. Not that that would have changed anything about your fate. But still there is an unpleasant aftertaste."

He pocketed the gun and left the house through the cellar door, which he carefully pulled close behind him.

„I completely forgot to tell him that he should not keep important documents so open" he murmured as he left the property at a leisurely pace.

46

Friday 6th May

At breakfast Yvonne showed MM her purchases with a proud face.

„You look like you're looking forward wearing the things you've bought. If that is indeed the case, I urgently ask you to revise your attitude. We are the victims of a filthy shabby blackmail and as soon as that is behind us, all this will be thrown away."

„Maybe you should see that a little bit more relaxed MM. Nothing bad has happened yet and probably your Mr. Triebel will soon find out who is behind it. So just try to enjoy the trip to Luxembourg."

MM looked at Yvonne with certain helplessness.

„Tell me now, if you like this crap really well!"

„There is something about it. Yes. You just have to have the courage to get involved in it."

The journey to Luxembourg had gone without a single word. She had already put on the 'gelle fra' dress at home. He had announced once again that he would wear the latex clothes only in his own garden and even for a single photo.

So, Yvonne stood with laurel wreath in front of the column 'gelle fra' and smiled into the camera while MM shot plenty of photos.

Then they went to the palace and photographed the square with palace in the background from all possible perspectives.

„I would like to sit in one of the cafes MM. What do you think?"

They sat in the warm sun.

„MM?" she looked at him innocently. „You have not talked to Triebel today. I would have thought that he is loitering somewhere."

MM leaned back in the chair with a complacent glance.

„That's what he is doing right now. But we have agreed absolute silence. After all, we do not know if he's listening to us or trying to locate the cell phones."

„Ah. And we expect Triebel's visit tonight?"

„That's the way it is. I am convinced that we will finally take a step forward. Therefore, unfortunately, we can not follow the advice of this miserable person and look around extensively in Luxembourg."

„There would be little time anyway. I do not get the photomontage that fast either. Should be as natural as possible after all."

MM looked at her blankly.

„Didn't you listen? We will meet with Triebel today and then the thing is finished."

„Then I do hope that not again any car thieves are on the way."

„If he again behaves so stupid, I will continue to work with Karlsson and Triebel can find a new client to earn money."

They were back in the early afternoon. The computer had received an e-mail. The blackmailer gave them until 8pm to send the two proof photos. It was not long before MM dialed the number of Triebel.

„I thought you had radio silence" Yvonne pointed out.

„Yes, but if this idiot does not come, then I'm probably forced to call him. Besides, I am back home and not in Luxembourg anymore."

Before Yvonne could answer, he was already yelling into the phone.

"Where are you staying Triebel?"

After that, MM became increasingly paler. Finally, he finished the conversation without saying another word.

„What's up MM?"

„I'll continue with Karlsson."

„Why? Did Triebel quit the job?"

„That's a way to express it."

Yvonne looked at him skeptically.

„You accept that just like that? You don't make a great deal out of it?"

„I have my reasons! And now we stop debating this subject. Looking forward is the order of the day."

Yvonne was even more skeptical, but then decided not to ask why Triebel was out of the race. The photo couldn't wait any longer.

„It's up to you. Get changed right now. In a minute you will be in your normal clothes again. And, the longer we delay, the worse the photomontage will be."

When MM finally stood completely in black in front of her, it was clear that MM had no sense of the indescribable feeling that the things had triggered in her brain. What a pity, as the blackmailer would have been disappointed about a MM with latex-fetish.

„You have to go to the garden. If I take a photo here, it will be noticed immediately."

He went morosely to the garden.

„You should not go as if you have a dozen raw eggs under your feet! Back straight and put on the heel first. That can not be that hard."

MM continued his unsteady gait.

„If you had told me that directly then I would have put them on in the garden. But you want to see me suffer!"

„I did not say anything else from the start, my dear MM" she replied with a smile, „only you had no interest in listening to me."

When he had finally positioned himself making as much fuss as possible, she photographed him several times with differently adjusted zoom factors. Then he let himself fall down in order to pull the boots off his feet.

As soon as he got back into his suit, he took the things and carried them towards the front door.

„What are you doing, MM?"

„Throwing it in the trash! What do you think?"

„I think that's a bad idea, because if you're unlucky, then I can't use the photos and you need to put the things back on."

He dropped everything where he stood and stomped toward the study.

„Do your very best. I do not want to put that on again!"

The door slammed shut.

„Sometimes my MM is a bit childish after all" Yvonne commented as she went into her study with a small smile to deal with the photomontage.

After some effort she had copied it into one of the pictures of the palace. On her first attempt, she realized with horror that MM was the only person without shadow. Since she did not know a program with which she could create a credible shadow, she chose a single person on the square and replaced it with the appropriately zoomed MM. In the format she chose, the color borders always blurred a bit. But finally, it fitted into the picture quite well.

MM just took a brief glance at her work, gave her a quick kiss as a 'thank you' and asked her to send the picture to the given mail address. The next thing she did was to clean the latex outfit. She played with the idea of making her daily cleaning and ironing a little more exciting by wearing these wonderful things.

Shortly after dinner came the answer mail from the blackmailer.

„Well done Yvonne. I did not want to see more.

MM, I'm wondering, if you think of me as a jerk. The photomontage is not bad, but it remains a montage. I presume you forced Yvonne to do it. So, I can't blame her. If you were so kind as to look at the pictures in the attachment?"

The two opened the attachment and saw themselves as they took the photos in front of the palace. It was crystal clear that MM could never have worn in the required outfit.

„You will understand that I could not do much with the photo. I have therefore decided to make it available to the general public. Please search the internet to find: 'man latex palace'.

If you were so kind as to produce the correct picture? Same address. You have 24 hours. Just that you do not get the idea to cheat again (unfortunately I can not be present to control you) it would be nice if Yvonne photographed you on the way from the parking garage at the "Place du Theater" to the

Palais. I want to see your complete body and your wonderful face on every photo. I think 10 nice pictures should be enough.

Then I would like to address something else. I finally found time to review the papers I took out of your safe. Of course, I immediately identified some of these as banknotes. (I hope, in your generosity, you will forgive me that I make a joke at this point. That raises the mood, especially in difficult situations). The other papers, however, have given a bit of a headache. I almost want to believe that they prove some fairly large tax-free businesses. Don't you know that something like that is forbidden? Also, I'm not sure if your business partners have so completely voluntarily agreed to do these businesses. As your dear friend I have to tell you that you can even be sentenced to prison. What if, by one brief moment inattentiveness, the papers end in wrong hands? E.g. the tax authority. Unthinkable.

Another short supplement. I really do not want that you bother strangers with your ridiculous problems. So, if you hire a new bastard with it, I can not guarantee that soon he will join Triebel and refuse any further cooperation."

MM said nothing for a long time. For a brief moment, Yvonne had the idea that he would lifelessly tip off the sofa the next moment.

„MM?"

„He is holding sway over me. Completely. If he passes on the documents, I'm done."

„And what about your new detective? Is he already on the way? Does he know someone who can find out the address behind the e-mail? Or can he even find out for himself?"

He looked at her uncomprehendingly.

„You know that I have no idea about such things. What do you mean? I do not see any address here!"

„Actually, rather simple. The computer from which the mail was sent has an unmistakable identity on the web. There is a way to get to the address of the guy who owns the computer. So far, at least I understand that. The problem is that only prosecution authorities have the opportunity to do so."

MM jumped up and disappeared into his study.

„What about the new photos?" Yvonne called after him.

„Shit! Shit! Shit! We have to do it!"

MM seemed anxious to spew his vocal cords along with the answer.

Saturday 7th May

In order not to have to change clothes in Luxembourg, MM was wearing the clothes under a pair of jeans and a shirt. The plan was to take the required photos as quickly as possible and to dress again with appropriate clothes right at the palace. MM had revived an old contact the day before. In exchange for a corresponding success fee, he got the promise to get the address associated with the e-mail within 48 hours. He had not understood much of what the hacker had told him about the job. In the end, that did not matter to him. For him, only one thing counted. The horror had to be ended.

In the parking garage, Yvonne made the first photo when leaving the car. On the way to the palace, she continued shooting photos. As Yvonne had expected, they got a lot of looks, but nobody really took offense at the action. MM was visibly under stress, but he also realized that in a few minutes everything would be over. He even made effort to walk rather steady despite the high heels.

Shortly before reaching their destination, it happened.

„Take a picture?" The voice came from a group of young Japanese tourists. Seconds later MM was surrounded by screeching Japanese. Everyone wanted to take a picture with him. Blocked by the high heels, MM had no chance to escape them. His, „No, no it's private", was not to be heard. After all, there was nothing left for him but to stand it. Everyone from the group posed with him. Some even pulled on the ring of his collar. The tour guide had retreated to a wall with a big smile. To MMs horror, she even made gestures that encouraged her group to take more pictures. MM looked around for Yvonne, but she seemed to be vanished.

Finally, he was so far back that he stood with his back to a wall, whereupon the tourist group shrieked even louder. Before he could wonder why, he noticed how a rope was pulled through his ring and knotted with a ring on the wall of the house. Now there were even more people gathering around him to take more pictures.

Then finally the interest in his person subsided and the group began to move again. One of the Japanese came back after a short time and handed him a 10€ note.

There was no sign of Yvonne. He suddenly realized he had no papers, no car keys, no money and no other clothes. Losing Yvonne had in no way been part of his plan.

„You need help Mister?" asked a familiar voice from behind.

„Yvonne, you're completely crazy? Didn't you see what happened to me? They nearly raped me!"

MM wanted to grab her and shake her. Only that would have gotten them even more attention.

„I had to buy new batteries. I could not help you against the Japanese anyway. When the camera went out of its own, I thought that I would at least use the time so that we could take the last picture at the palace."

Only with difficulty he could control himself.

„Did you see what these idiots did to me? A few of them would have liked to pull me around like a pet."

Yvonne drew his attention to the people who had stopped to watch the entertaining act with the Japanese and were now curious to see if the show went any further.

„I would suggest that we quickly walk to the Palais. Then you can put on your shirt and pants. If we stop here for a long time, it can only get worse."

He had no choice but to agree. Some time later she had actually taken the last picture and MM walked in plain clothes back to the car.

„Never in my life I will visit this cursed city again. Imagine what would have happened if I had lost you. I had nothing at all. Sooner or later I would have been arrested."

Yvonne let him swear for a while. He finally had experienced a lot. She only hoped that he would not come up with the idea of wondering what would happen to all the pictures the Japanese made.

Sunday 8th May

„Why didn't you do it straight away like that? I'll call you again tomorrow. Have a great day."

When the phone rang, MM learned that the hacker had found out the address. A little later, Karlsson stood at the door. Like Triebel, Karlsson also worked with very few staff and had already handled some questionable missions. In contrast to Triebel, Yvonne had the unmistakable impression that Karlsson was a stupid thug. He set off with MM immediately on the way to the address where they suspected the blackmailer.

A few hours later, Yvonne received another mail.

„Dear MM. Why did you have to scare this honorable old lady?

Having given you enough chance to follow my rules, you taxed my patience long enough.

But one by one:

First our little e-mail correspondence:
Of course, I'm not presumptuous to consider myself as flawless actor, but to send mails via my own account ... Excuse me, I'm not that stupid. However, I have to pay respect, that you found the address. Although that was probably one of your dubious friends again. However. The lady did not even know that she has an e-mail address at all. Anyway, I suspect that because this address was not used for months. Probably one of the dear children has set up the computer.

I assure that this trail cannot lead to me. Incidentally, finding the address I'm using now is also wasted time.

The end of my patience:
Of course, it's a little problem for me. If I simply pass the documents on to the prosecutor, you will get some big problems, but then I can not be the thorn in your side any longer. So, I will choose an interim solution. Not completely harmless, but since nothing really bad can happen (at least not me), if it goes wrong, I'll let it happen.

The next game:
It starts with a time gap. In other words: You probably can live one week on your own. Because of the above announced intermediate solution, I need a little time. I hope you are not too disappointed."

Yvonne read the mail several times. The blackmailer gave MM a whole week to catch his breath and get everything he needed to find him. The blackmailer seemed to underestimate MM.

In the late afternoon MM returned with Karlsson. After the two had read the mail, they clapped each other off and recalled again the most beautiful scenes with the old woman.

Yvonne looked at them in horror.

„Don't you feel sorry for the old woman? What are you doing when she reports to the police?"

„Nonsense. She could not recognize us. We were only briefly in the apartment. She only stood in the corner and held her hands in front of the face. Maybe she was scared that we would beat her."

Karlsson beamed all over his face.

„Why does she let strangers into her house? Do not worry Yvonne. Even if she calls the police, they can't get us."

MM gave her a kiss on the cheek.

„If you excuse us now please? The jerk leaves us a whole week to corner him. We won't let that chance unused."

The two disappeared into MMs study and left the speechless Yvonne alone. When she went to bed late at night, she could still hear them debating.

Monday 9th May

It was like the blackmailer had suspected. After the old lady had recovered from the shock the two masked ruffians had inflicted on her, she had called her daughter. She literally lived at the other end of the world and therefore could not come herself to help her mother, but she informed the German police about the incident. They sent a young policewoman to find out what really had happened.

Since the policewoman herself had a grandmother at the age of the victim, the two women quickly got in touch with each other. Finally, the old woman showed her a laptop. It was kept safely in a cupboard in the lower drawer and would probably have stayed there for a long time. But now the two ruffians had visited her.

When the policewoman opened the mail-box, she found an e-mail that had just arrived a few hours ago. The text was read quickly: „*Good luck*"

Attached were two pictures. One showed a tall man 'type doormen' walking toward the old woman's house. In the corner of the photo was a small part of a black car. From the height of the fender that could actually be a SUV. The second photo showed the complete SUV with clearly recognizable number plate. The photo was made in the same street as she could see on the background. After the old woman took her glasses, she confirmed that the man depicted was one of the two ruffians. She was surprised, however, that no image of the second man was there.

„Did they touch anything here in the apartment?" the policewoman wanted to know.

„Yes, but they were wearing black gloves. I do not think you can find fingerprints here young woman."

„You never know. People often leave more tracks than they think. I will show the photos to my boss right away. If this is no photomontage, then we'll get them."

Meanwhile, the table was set and the two had coffee and cake.

„What did the second man look like?"

„Hard to say. I did not see any faces. He was definitely not as strong and tall as the first man. He was rather slim. He also seemed to have long hair. Today, some men wear a ponytail."

„Why do you think he had a ponytail?"

„At the back of his cap, a tuft of hair was barely covered. That seemed to be a ponytail."

„You observed very well. Maybe that will help."

She took another piece of the cake.

„Really delicious."

„Thank you very much. I always have some cake in the house. You never know if a surprise visit will come."

Terrified, she put her hand at her mouth.

„Of course, I did not mean a visit, like that of the two ruffians."

„I got it", the policewoman reassured her. „What exactly happened when the two came to your apartment?"

„Very easily. They rang the bell and then came in without asking for permission. The doorman-guy pushed me into the corner and they started asking where my computer was."

„And? Did you show them the laptop?"

„No. I was too excited to think about the laptop. Besides, they said 'computer'. I think they soon noticed that they were wrong."

„That is, they did not even try to take any valuables with them? Money? Jewelry? Something like that?"

„No. Nothing. They started directly with the questioning about the computer and some of the things that I should have sent. I think they called it 'mals'. Something like this."

„E-mails. That's the term for electronic mail. Like the one we opened some minutes ago", the policewoman explained. „I will check to whom the car belongs. After that, the gentleman will be visited by one of my colleagues."

„That is, you will soon have the ruffians?"

There was a little hope in the old woman's voice.

„Looks like."

***

At about the same time, Karlsson looked at his screen in disbelief.

„Dear Mr. Karlsson,

I have allowed myself to put a small photo gallery on the Internet. Attached to this mail you will find a selection of pictures. I do not want to give the impression of being in love with myself, but I can not avoid looking at the pictures in quality and high level of detail as little masterpieces. Also, if this is not formally tenable, since I can not pride myself of having been awarded the title of "Master of the photographic craft" by any artists' association.

But I move away from the topic and let me take away into the darkest sides of bloviating. Though it has a liberating effect for every persons mind it can also lead to wasting valuable time. In that case, your time is very limited Mr. Karlsson.

‚Why my time?' you will perhaps ask annoyed. After all, only someone photographed me while visiting an old lady and now tries to create blackmail in a bungling way. Absolutely no sign of time trouble.

Well, respected Mr. Karlsson. I also emailed two of the pictures to the old lady. Not that I think she would unpack her laptop and open her mailbox now. No, that certainly will not happen. But I'm pretty sure this was done by the police officer who yesterday gave herself the honor to visit the old lady relatively soon after you and your friend, the highly respected MM did so.

In his eternal self-centeredness MM will have failed to point out that I'm not a friend of his tendency to ask for help while he is investigating who I might be. So please be a well-educated boy and quit your job in the service of MM."

„The guy is completely crazy. That's sick. Against such people reasonably thinking people are always at a disadvantage!"

„Do you want to turn tail just because he uploaded a few images?"

MM had fallen from all the clouds when Karlsson had reported by phone.

„Of course, I do not turn tail, but it would have been advisable if you had explained a bit better about the guy. Nevertheless, you will have to work without me for a few days."

MM could not believe his ears.

„You get good money! Who do you think you are? You will take care of the blackmail and nothing else. Is that clear?"

„Just forget it." Karlsson continued unperturbed. „If I walk that easy into a trap during my work and then must reckon with the visit of the police, then I always take a break with the case. Get distance is top priority now."

„I double your money. Now get down to work. We speak as agreed this evening."

When MM said that, his tone made clear that no contradiction was tolerated.

„Alright MM. You have money without limits and you think that you can buy everything. But guys like me, we have principles. You know? I do it the way I just told you. After that you are free to ask me again. I'm willing to work for a higher commission."

Tuesday 10th May

„How does it go, MM?"

„Everything is under control. Very soon the last curtain will fall."

MM made every effort to sound confident. It was harder than he thought, but worth the effort, because he could see in Yvonne's face that she believed him.

„I thought that Karlsson would come to a briefing yesterday. In a way, I'm also affected."

MM gently caressed her cheek.

„I know, but that's a man's business. You are already too much involved in the problems."

„Don't worry about that. I think it's a very interesting distraction from everyday life."

„Distraction from everyday life? Someone wants to knock me down and you call that an interesting distraction?"

„Don't get upset. You just told me that you have everything under control. Otherwise I would have never thought about it in that way."

He looked at his watch. She already knew what was coming „Okay, I have to go now."

Half an hour later, Yvonne had slipped on the latex clothes and tottered through the house with her high heeled boots trying to do her housework. Still, the distraction was not big enough to stop her thoughts from straying. She could not forgive him the trip to the old woman. Besides, she had the feeling that he was not upfront with her about Triebel. The more she thought about it, the bigger grew the distance she felt between herself and MM.

She was still thinking about it when the doorbell rang. As Yvonne was busy in the hall, she opened the door without thinking, and faced a tall man and a small woman she had not seen before. The surprised faces of the two, and the fresh air streaming over her body, reminded Yvonne of the clothes she was wearing.

„Yes?" It's best to pretend that nothing special is going on. That's what Beatrice taught her.

The woman tried to fall back in routine. She presented herself as Inspector Smidt and her colleague as DS Rednich. Both showed their ID-Cards.

„May we come in for a moment?"

Automatically Yvonne stepped aside and made a welcoming gesture towards the living room.

The Inspector opened the conversation.

„I want to be straightforward. We investigate in a murder case."

She took the time to watch the reaction on Yvonne's face. In fact, Yvonne needed a moment to catch herself. She hoped that the police would not tell her that her own husband was the murder case.

„Who?"

„Do not worry; it's nobody from your family circle. Your husband and according to the documents also you yourself, had contact to a detective agency Triebel. Is that correct?"

„Yes, he often worked for my husband."

„You use the past tense?"

„My husband tells very little about his work. I only know that he has now switched to another detective agency. Besides, you've just told me yourself that you're investigating a murder case. Then it is obvious that it is Triebel."

„Right. It is actually Triebel. Why did your husband change the detective agency?"

„That's best to ask my husband. As I said, he does not really tell much about his activities."

She got one of MMs business cards from a drawer.

„I'm just the woman at his side. Nothing more."

The two automatically looked meaningfully at her outfit again.

„Don't you sweat in these things?"

„Yes, but it is still a great feeling. Besides, it does not really matter to you what I'm wearing in my own four walls. If I would have been naked, you would probably have to accept it in the same way as any other clothing."

„Excuse me. Of course, you are right. I was just eager to learn about it."

The Inspector realized that she blushed.

Yvonne realized that she felt somewhat superior to her.

„I can recommend a shop here in the city, where you can get really very attentive advice."

„No thanks" the Inspector waved. „As I said: just curious."

The two made preparations to get on their way again.

„You probably can not really help us. Thank you for your husband's business card. However, there are already colleagues of ours with him. Maybe he can give us more information."

„You haven't told me how he died."

„He was found dead in his house. We can't say more than that. Although it seems to be a fact that you have nothing to do with the murder, we can't tell you more about it."

When Yvonne was alone again, she realized how a huge inner tension fell.

MMs ashen face in the telephone conversation with Triebel, the warnings that the blackmailer had written in the mails. Should she have had to show the mails to the police? Had she kept something from them? She came to the conclusion that they simply asked the wrong questions. Without lying to the police, she had concealed the basics. If she had previously known about the visit, the conversation would certainly have been different. She would have worn other clothes and therefore it would probably have come to other questions. Now she had played her part in the blackmail affair in a way she had never imagined.

She wondered if it was her job to alert MM, then decided against it. After all, he had kept her in the dark about the death of Triebel, and he already seemed to have a visit from the police. What was she supposed to warn him about?

In the afternoon she decided to make a little trip to the city. Maybe it would help to switch her thoughts to something different. She walked aimlessly through the streets and looked at the shops. Without wanting it directly, she eventually came to Beatrice's shop.

„I'm glad that you come here again."

Beatrice came towards her beaming with joy.

„I was just nearby and thought, I'll just come in for a short stay."

„I am glad. What was your husband's reaction?"

Yvonne shook her head.

„Let's talk about something else. I can't understand how someone can react that stupid. The things are so fantastic."

„You can't force people to do what is good for them."

She looked regretfully at Yvonne.

„And? What are you doing with the things now?"

„I decided to wear it. In the morning, when I'm doing the cores, I am always alone. I wear the things and of course the cool boots."

Beatrice's eyes grew wider.

„Really? Well, then I hope that you do not get a problem with the lock again."

Automatically, Yvonne scanned Beatrice for locks, but could not find one.

„No, not today, that would be boring."

Beatrice scanned the store.

„What would you like to try today?"

„You tell me."

„Have you ever thought about a corset? You have exactly the figure for it."

Yvonne looked at her own body.

„Well, thank you. Until now I thought that my body is in a good shape."

„That's what it is. A corset would flatter your figure a little bit. Optimize curves that already exist. Something completely else with fat people. When they put on a corset, they always expect to get an hourglass-figure."

Yvonne looked blankly at Beatrice. So she had to explain a little more.

„The whole fat doesn't fly away, just because you strap a corset around it. People like you can really wear something like this. Just come with me. I will show you."

After Beatrice had closed the lacing, Yvonne made some cautious moves.

„Not as bad as I thought. I think I could even wear it while cleaning."

In response, Beatrice opened the door to a small chamber and took out a broom and a dustpan.

„Try it."

Yvonne was so surprised that she automatically received the two pieces.

„Where should I start?"

„Actually, I meant it as a joke, but if you ask, just sweep through the entire sales room."

With that Beatrice left her alone and took care of the clientele. Yvonne turned to the showroom after a brief hesitation. A few minutes later, she realized that this was exactly the task she needed to settle down and forget all the stress with MM. When she finished the room, more than an hour had passed. She had automatically started dusting the shelves after sweeping.

„Can you tell me when this room was thoroughly cleaned the last time? Actually, you could book me directly for a whole week if you want to have the store really clean."

„To be honest. The former cleaning lady quitted last week and I haven't found anything new. But from time to time I sweep by myself."

Yvonne again pointedly watched the room.

„I do not want to offend you, but to be straight, I would say that you definitely have no talent for cleaning."

„I know." After a short break, Beatrice added: „Did you really mean that? Your offer to be cleaning woman?"

Yvonne did not need to think twice.

„Sure, I can do it. Such a shop just has to be clean."

„But you do not need that. I thought your husband has a hell of a lot of money?"

„Yes. But on the same high level he's a pain in my neck. Why shouldn't I start a small underpaid second job?"

„Your decision." Beatrice took a contract from a drawer. „The cleaning staff always gets a standard contract with me", she explained, pushing the paper to Yvonne.

„Read it and sign it."

The contract specified working hours and pay in the usual legal jargon. For Yvonne, the money was not important at all. The work clothes were provided by the employer. So she did not have to take any aprons or the like from home. She signed and pushed the contract back to Beatrice.

„When should I start?"

Beatrice looked at her slightly amused.

„You did not really read that, did you? Tomorrow afternoon at two o'clock. You stay until four. This applies to all days from Monday to Saturday. If you can't do it on one or the other day let me know and we'll just postpone it. Since tomorrow is your first day, it would be quite good if you can come an hour earlier."

A short time later, Yvonne stood on the street wearing her new corset. She had not dared to keep the item directly, but Beatrice had convinced her that it would be best if she did not even bother to show herself in public. Besides, she still wore a jacket. This covered the most anyway. Yvonne had noticed immediately how her posture changed. Simultaneously with the attitude, something like a strengthened self-confidence flowed into her.

Yvonne had been shown how to tie the lacing on the back even without help. In the next few days she would have plenty of opportunity to practice that.

Wednesday 11th May

„MM? I had a visit from the police yesterday."

„Me too. Imagine, they just came to my company. They treated me like a criminal. Of course I immediately told them that without my lawyer I could not make any statement about Triebel. I have no idea why they asked me? How could I have any idea who might have killed Triebel."

And again one level lower in the scale, flashed through Yvonne's mind. Ridiculous. MM wanted to tell her that he saw no connection between the blackmail and Triebel's death.

„Do you remember that the blackmailer threatened not to bring in any strangers?"

The disdain was in MMs face, even before he opened his mouth.

„Do not always be so ridiculous! The blackmailer is a poor madman. Admittedly he's causing me more problems than I expected, but that's not why he's a cold-blooded murderer. Triebel finally had other cases to look after. Should the police poke around there. Let them find a promising approach in that area."

He took his briefcase

„I wish a pleasant day and do not rack your brain about what had happened to Triebel! Your job is to be beautiful. It's just that simple."

With that he disappeared towards his company.

Later in the morning, another mail from the blackmailer came in. After the put-down she had received in the morning, Yvonne could not help to have a certain joyful anticipation when opening it.

„I'm so far done with my little additional jobs. Now I have time for our little game again. Earlier than expected. I bet you are happy. The rules remain the same. You can still exit by making a self-denunciation. But I personally believe that you are not ready for that.

I repeat again that I do not like it, if you get foreign help. So please just stop it. It's bad enough that Yvonne has to help you.

Your next destination you should head with the plane. Otherwise, the journey takes just too long. The city is the largest of its country and quite old. I'm not sure if the great Julius was there in person, but there are signs. The city already existed, though the name was different. Yvonne, would you be so kind to photograph MM when he gets on the tram that's known far beyond the city limits? His new nose piercing - I suggest septum - should be clearly visible. Please choose a ring with at least one centimeter inside diameter. You are welcome to choose a bigger MM. You can leave your beloved latex outfit at home. Jeans and denim jacket are enough. But please take care that your entire garments have clear signs of wear. Of course after the shooting the piercing stays at its place. You're just getting used to it.

You may also take a picture of Yvonne again. Actually two. One on entering a barbershop with her currently blond hair. Another when leaving the salon with black hair. The choice of the new cut is up to you Yvonne. You and the creativity of the hairdresser will do it.

Tomorrow, you have time to prepare. Please book the flight for Friday morning. I will write tomorrow, how we will make contact there. Return flight not before Sunday evening."

Yvonne could not help laughing. If she had a glass in her hand, she would surely have raised it. Her MM, the man who took off his suit only to sleep and shower. Her MM with clearly visible piercing and worn jeans. She would not be surprised if he came up with the idea to ask for a crease on his jeans. She picked up the phone.

„MM, we got another mail."

„I wonder why you always get away so well Yvonne. Dyeing hair is not really a pain. Me, on the other hand..."

He reached for a glass of hard liquor.

„The day I catch him will be the day, when he regrets to be born at all."

In his face Yvonne could see every single torment that he would cause to the blackmailer. She didn't know what to think about it.

„How far did you move forward with your research?"

MM looked past her out of the window.

„It does not work out as I had imagined. Karlsson turned tail after the blackmailer denounced him to the police. Of course, I told him that he won't get any payment for his service, but that did not change his mind."

MM nodded silently. Then he banged his fist on the table.

„But that will not make me let this person do what he wants. Did you already figured out where he wants to send us this time?"

Yvonne produced an illustrated book.

„With Julius, I thought of Julius Caesar. If that is correct then it can only be a city in the Mediterranean, plus Paris and London."

„At 'tram', you think about Lisbon?" MM wanted to know.

Meanwhile Yvonne had turned the matching page.

„Exactly. Lisbon is the capital, is the largest city and was called 'Felicitas Julia' at Julius times. I think that we have the city, or do you remember another capital with a famous tram?"

„No, the only other famous tram I can think of is in San Francisco. Forget it. Due to the age. Much to young. Otherwise, the other cities have famous subways."

Yvonne looked at MM.

„And now?"

„What 'and now?' "

„What do we do now? I quickly get the required items. And a few others that you can travel with too. What I meant is whether we fly to Lisbon on Friday and then if we do what he wants or if we stay here and take the chance that you get him fast enough."

MM said nothing for a long time. Finally, he took Yvonne's hands.

„I've spent the last two days picking out some of those with whom I've done business. Business that can be called illegal or at least: on the edge of legality."

He paused.

„Nothing. Absolutely nothing. I didn't get it. None of them reacted in any way to the remarks that I put into the talks. So, I'm still at the very beginning."

„Not really" Yvonne corrected „After all, you can drop some names from the list."

MM managed to toss her a brief smile.

„Right. On the other hand, those were the prime suspects. What's left are the more harmless cases."

„Also business partners?"

MM shook his head.

„No, these are the ones from whom I have taken companies or company shares. I lost contact after the transactions. I would be surprised if it is one of them."

„After all, you took away parts of their company", Yvonne objected.

First she got a blank look then MM started laughing.

„I saved them from worse. When I consider that some of those idiots probably did not recognize yet, that I was the cause of their problems..."

Maybe, Yvonne thought, those are exactly the ones you should be looking for my dear MM.

She just wanted to point it out when he got up and disappeared into his study without further words.

Why, asked Yvonne herself, did I think that he really wanted to talk with me?

Disappointed she took a few women's magazines and studied hairstyles. Why not a short haircut? Maybe a pixie haircut? The drying of the long hair has been annoying for a long time. Finally she tore out some pages with matching hairstyles and, as a precaution, packed them in her handbag.

***

Precisely at 1pm Yvonne stood in Beatrice' shop.

„Nice that you are on time", she was greeted by Beatrice. „The best we go right back and see if you fit into the clothes."

When Yvonne saw what had been put out to her, she sank dumbfounded on a chair and looked wide-eyed between Beatrice and the garments.

„I was thinking of an apron and gloves."

„I do not understand that an intelligent woman like you can sign a work contract she has not completely read. But you signed it and now you have to go through it", Beatrice told her with a smile. „After all, you can keep the things if you've worked here long enough."

Yvonne needed a short moment to suck it up. Then she stood up determined.

„Where can I change?"

„Right here I would suggest. I have to give you one or the other tip."

After Yvonne had undressed, she reached for the stockings. Beatrice held her back.

„The best, you put on the string thong first."

Next piece was a corset. Beatrice helped her lacing it up. It was as tight as the one she had bought the previous day.

„Now you are almost done. Only attach the stockings to the straps."

Beatrice handed her the pair of shiny black stockings and a small, tube-shaped structure, which she could put on as a dress.

„Sit down, I'll help with the boots. We needed a little bit longer than I thought. Your working hours will start in a few minutes."

Yvonne was so overwhelmed with her outfit that she did not pay any attention to what boots were put on her. It was not until she heard two locks snap in. Then she noticed the extremely high stiletto heels.

„You're serious? I hope you have the right keys too?"

„Of course. I have. That's part of it. Just stand up", Beatrice asked as she reached behind herself. „Now the gloves."

She put on black latex gloves, which reached to the middle of her upper arms.

„Perfect. Take a look at the mirror."

Yvonne was struck all of a heap. The clothes had changed her into another woman.

„Now all that is missing is the corresponding make-up and one or the other piece of jewelry, then I think nobody would recognize me anymore."

„Right. You can put on make-up over there. Then you come to me in the sales room. I'll give you the matching jewelry."

With that, Beatrice left her alone. A few minutes later, a perfectly made-up Yvonne joined her.

„Do you like it?"

„Wow. You really understand to achieve the maximum effect with minimal effort. Maybe you should rather make your money as a make-up artist instead of cleaning stuff."

„Thank you. I'll think about it, but first I'm under contract in your shop and it seems to me, the job will have a few surprises for me and won't be boring at all. That's the main thing."

„That's a reasonable attitude. Bend over to me, I still have the promised jewelry for you."

Yvonne heard the click of a lock again. In the mirror, she realized that she now wore shiny stainless-steel collar. It had a large ring, which she automatically grasped with thumb and forefinger and moved up and down.

„I think you should start cleaning now. Actually, you're already half an hour late."

„Actually, I am no longer surprised that you have problems finding new cleaning women."

Beatrice smiled.

„We can talk about that later. Now I have to earn some money again and you can do your favorite activity and clean my shop."

When Yvonne already turned away, Beatrice gave her the tip not to be irritated by the customers sayings.

72

Thursday 12ᵗʰ May

„Please get everything we need and book a top hotel in Lisbon."

Yvonne frowned: „You're sure about the top hotel?"

MM gave her an irritated look as he was about to leave the room.

„You think, I'm broke? You're wrong! Of course you'll book a top hotel."

With that statement, he left her. Yvonne looked for a hotel with the requested standards. She booked the 'Real Palacio'. Let's see how the master will perform with the jewelry on his nose and the rundown clothes.

Then she went shopping again. In corset and high heels, she felt like a pop star enjoying a relaxed morning. In a second-hand shop, she got the pants, the jacket and some T-shirts that had already seen better days. After that she bought some new jeans and shirts. That should do it for MM.

After she had stowed her shopping in the car, it was time to do her cleaning job at Beatrice' shop. The change was much faster this time. The only problem was that the store was much better visited this time.

At the 'cleaning job closing time' - coffee – as Yvonne called it - she questioned Beatrice about that.

„Don't you think it's better if I clean before opening. Today, the customers kept getting in the way."

„That's out of question. The business went really well today and what do you think, what I sold best?"

Yvonne shrugged her shoulders.

„No idea."

„Of course, just the clothes and accessories that you have worn today."

„You're joking, right?"

„No. You're the absolute bestseller. I'm sure my customers are starting word-of-mouth recommendation. That's fantastic."

„Then you will not like to hear that I'm going to Lisbon with my husband for a few days."

73

„And what about your cleaning job? You have signed a contract!"

„Now do not get upset. You have already made more profit today than you pay me for wages. That's at least what you told me right now. Besides, that's just for the weekend." After a short break, she concretized. „long weekend to be honest. It starts tomorrow morning. On Monday I'll be again your sales-increasing cleaning lady."

„How do you want to balance that?"

Beatrice had a disappointed pitch in her voice.

„No idea. I'll stay a few additional hours next week until I've balanced the two days."

„Would be a possibility. But maybe I can think of something else too. We will see."

When Yvonne started to leave, the question that she feared came up.

„Does your husband have business appointments in Lisbon where he wants to shine with a beautiful woman by his side?"

„No. He is in a very difficult situation and I am almost obligated to help him."

Beatrice looked questioningly at Yvonne.

„I do not have to understand that right now, right?"

„No. That's actually pretty complicated. The less people know about it, the better."

Friday 13th May

A bright blue sky welcomed them in Lisbon. MM had barely exchanged a word with Yvonne throughout the flight. She herself, has had no interest in addressing him to the upcoming events. After coming home the night before, they had had a fierce debate. Yvonne even had thought about sleeping in a separate room. She still did not see at all that he constantly blamed her for his failures. After all, she was drawn in it completely innocent.

The blackmailer had again reported and as announced a new mail address specified. At the same time, he had apologized with an accustomed convolution that he had forgotten to point out to MM that he should open his beloved ponytail for the photo and add some colorful hairspray. The requested photos should be sent on Friday evening. For Saturday he had announced a mail with further tasks. Which tasks that would depend on how good the photos would be.

Now they had dropped their luggage in their rooms and headed to downtown Lisbon. The only thing Yvonne was curious about was how MM wanted to solve the situation.

Using the service of the hotel, Yvonne had already booked a hairdresser. Her appointment was scheduled at 3 o'clock in the afternoon. So they had enough time for a little stroll through the old town. MM used this to buy green hairspray in a drugstore. After some searching, he finally found a shop where he could buy fake piercing jewelry that looked deceptively real. So he wanted to start the big bluff again. MM saw her skeptical look.

„Do you think, I will start some self-mutilation? If you keep your fingernails, that's up to you. In any case, I play the game according to my rules. And piercing myself is not part of it."

They had arrived near the tram line. He held out the spray can. „If you would be so kind?"

Without a word she took it and dyed his hair green. Some passers-by took this opportunity to stay. However, the attention was not as big as a few days ago in Luxembourg. When a tram stopped, he stuck his piercing to the nasal septum and made preparations to get on the tram while she took the requested pictures. There was some relief in his gaze, when he dropped the piercing jewelry into a waste bin.

They were good at time to get to the barber on time.

„If you do not want to, you can also put on a wig." MM offered unexpectedly. Actually, she had expected that nothing could be more important to him than to get the color out of his hair.

„Just let me have a go. I'm doing that right. As with the fingernails. I have no idea when you'll finally catch him and, most of all, I have no idea what he's capable of. In fact, unlike you, I believe he is involved in the death of Triebel. That's why I do not want to get into his line of fire. Not as long as he does not demand anything impossible from me."

„And what would be impossible for you?"

MM studied the map and tried to keep his orientation.

„No idea, I'll might see it then. Should I tell you now that I would not kill anyone if he asked me to?"

MM didn't answer. Yvonne wondered if he even heard her answer. Maybe he had lost orientation? This old town seemed to be too narrow for MM. A glance at the clock showed her that they only had 10 minutes left.

„Maybe a taxi?"

MM looked at her confused.

„No, no. Not necessary."

He pointed to the end of the small alley.

„It must be there behind the corner."

He was right. At 3 o'clock she entered the barbershop. MM had taken the picture and now went down to the sea to wash the color out of his hair. They had agreed that it would make no sense if he came back before 5 o'clock.

After some searching, he found a spot where he was somewhat out of sight. Since he would throw away the rundown clothes anyway, he went a bit into the sea, to be able to immerse his head. When he realized that someone was standing behind him, a long, pointed knife was already held in front of his face.

„Don't move!"

This request MM would not have needed at the moment, because out of sheer terror he was paralyzed. Another hand held out a pair of sunglasses

„Take this!"

When he had them on, he noticed that the glasses were blackened. Instinctively, he tried to look past the edge, but found that the glasses were close to his face and the eyeglass temple were so wide that even at the side was nothing to see.

„Come!"

He was taken by the arm and led out of the water. Presumably not to attract attention, one arm was placed around his shoulder. This made the way across the beach to the road a bit shaky. Passers-by might have to have the impression that there were a few drunken buddies on the way to the nearest pub. His green hair would have stopped even the few attentive people from helping him. Maybe they even thought he was captured by his social worker. When they reached the street, he was shoved in a car. From the way they got in, that had to be at least a minibus. After being placed on a bench, his hands were handcuffed. When he finally began to think again, he realized that he could no longer be led like a lamb to the slaughter. He was still able to attract the attention of passers-by. He put all his strength into his voice.

He managed only one pitiful weak sound, because something big round was stuck in his wide opened mouth. Before he could shake his head or push the foreign matter out with his tongue, he realized that the part was attached to a strap that was tightly fastened at the back of his head.

From satisfied little laughs, he concluded that his kidnappers congratulated themselves on gagging him so quickly. Hoping to have one last chance, MM jumped up and tried to escape in the direction in which he suspected the door. Immediately, several strong hands pushed him back onto the bench. Afterwards, a foul-smelling cloth was held in front of his nose. 'Chloroform' shot through his mind, then his resistance got rapidly weaker.

***

After two relaxing hours in the barbershop, Yvonne stepped back into the street. She had needed a bit, but finally she had agreed with the maestro, as he called himself, on a spicy crop with hinted broad mohawk stripe. Since the lateral hair was not down shaved, the cut seemed quite sociable. The mohawk had only come to her mind at the last moment because she wanted to annoy MM a little bit.

But now there was no sign of MM. She figured he'd probably gone to the hotel after washing out the green paint to get a decent dress. His cell phone answered with the mailbox. Actually strange, she thought, because if he had gone to the hotel, then the cell phone would certainly be the first part he would have taken back. She decided to give him another fifteen minutes and then return to the hotel herself. In the meantime, she took some selfies with the barbershop in the background. After all, she wanted to avoid additional stress with the blackmailer. He would probably take a closer look at the photo of MM. Then he would notice that he hadn't followed the instructions once again.

***

MM had seen the last hours as through a fog. His kidnappers had always forced him to sniff so much that he was turned off but not completely kicked out. When peace finally set in, he lay horizontally and could not move. He had a headache and did not know if he had to vomit. Fortunately, the gag had been taken out. So, he did not have to worry about suffocating on his own vomit.

Since he could not see anything, he tried to hear his surroundings. He could not notice anything special. He had always heard that in such situations the sense of time could get lost. Now he realized that was true. The mere fact that he felt hungry was an indication that the evening had already begun.

***

At the front desk they had not seen MM and also in their rooms was no trace. Normally, the worn jeans should have been in the trash or on the bathroom floor. Yvonne did not know if she should be seriously worried about MM now or if he might have found a hot lead to the blackmailer. He would also have been able to recruit detectives to investigate him and the surrounding area for conspicuous persons. After yesterday's argument, she would not have been angry with him if he had kept that secret. She initially decided not to do anything. In Portugal, as in Germany, the search for missing adults would presumably begin no sooner than 24 hours after their disappearance. Yvonne suggested that this deadline would probably be extended in her case. She imagined the conversation with the police.

„Has there been any argument with your husband lately?"
„Yeah, I would have preferred to leave him last night."
The police officers would look meaningful.
„What brings you to Lisbon?"
„Oh, you know, my husband did tons of illegal business. Now someone who has blackmailed him has come to grips with it. If the materials, the blackmailer has in his hands, come to the public, my husband will probably go to jail for a few years."
„We will do what we can and of course contact the German authorities immediately. They then have to decide if they want to do something about the blackmail."

It definitely was not like that. If so, then she had to come up with a story that came across reasonably believable.

„Has there been any argument with your husband lately?"

79

„We have been a heart and a soul for years. He reads every wish from my eyes."

If Yvonne smoked, now would be the time to take a cigarette and try to use the lighter with shaky hands. Of course, the police would jump at her rescue immediately and with a steady hand hold the lighter.

„What brings you to Lisbon?"

„This is our anniversary. We always go to Portugal at this time. Sometimes in the south, sometimes in the north. This time we chose Lisbon."

„How come that they booked last night?"

Tears would probably not help her now. Conceived stories often have a hard time in reality.

Finally, she started the laptop and sent the photos to the address she had received yesterday. After just a few minutes, the answer came:

„Thanks for the photos.

Yvonne, you did exactly the thing I asked for. MM, however, still believes that my instructions may be interpreted. By now you will have realized that he has not returned to the hotel. He will not make it to the hotel any more. But I can assure you that he will be at the airport early enough to take the return flight with you. I have no other tasks for you. Just enjoy the time in Lisbon. This is a really nice place."

Saturday 14ᵗʰ May

When MM woke up, he did not know how many times he had already awakened from sleep. The headache had gone and he had total control over his mind. Only he still could not see anything because he was still blindfolded. Shackles left him only a minimum of movement. He was lying in a bed. His feet and hands were tied to the bed with strong shackles at their respective corners. Even around his neck he felt a bondage, which seemed to be nowhere attached. He had the feeling that because of the long fixation he had no muscle in his body that did not hurt.

When the door opened, he winced. On the one hand something would happen now, on the other hand he was afraid of what the kidnappers would do to him.

Several people seemed to be around his bed.

„Don't make wrong!"

Even for his German ears, this was bad English, but at least it was English and not Portuguese. He nodded to signal that he understood. He was then taken to the toilet. The collar he wore around his neck was used to make every attempt to fight them impossible. Apparently, they had hooked a pole, so as not to give it the chance to somehow get too close to one of the kidnappers. When he had just got up from bed and tried to get his limbs moving again, he realized that he had not a single piece of close on his body. The attempt to cover himself with his hands was received by his kidnappers with much laughter. A short time later, his hands were tied behind his back.

After the toilet he got water to drink. He could only hope that the water contained no additives, but he also knew that denying would have done nothing, since the kidnappers could probably also let him die of thirst. Besides, what should he do with his hands bound and his eyes blindfolded, except to put the kidnappers in a bad mood? He had no choice but to wait for his chance.

He was taken to another room and seated on a chair that reminded him of a dentist's dental chair. When his hands, legs and arms were tied to separate supports, he discarded the dentist's chair and replaced it with the gynecological chair. To his horror, the criminals could now swing and lock his arms and legs as they pleased. When he wanted to straighten up, he was also fixed with the collar. Like the whole night before, he was completely fixed again. Only he was not alone this time.

„What do you want from me?"

Speaking should be the best thing to do in such situations. He had read that anyway. As it seemed, the kidnappers probably knew that too.

„Quiet!"

„But I help. I have money!"

This time he got the gag back in his mouth as an answer. He heard someone handling things like he was preparing some kind of medical treatment. Finally, someone put his face in his hands and bent his head toward the neck.

„Don't move."

Someone got on his nose. After a short time, a clamp was put on the nasal septum. When he realized that now apparently the piercing should be done, that the blackmailer had demanded, he tried desperately to turn his head away. One of the kidnappers grunted morosely. Another seemed to be happy. After that, his head was fixed with some straps so strong that he could make no further movements. It came as he expected. A stabbing pain shot through his body as the needle was pushed through. After some fumbling the pressure disappeared and he realized that he was wearing a ring in his nose, which he could easily reach with his upper lip. But instead of loosening the fixation, they tampered with his ear. His tormentors slowly worked their way up his ear. He counted ten rings. After that, his head was finally freed again. MM became more and more aware of how helpless he was at the mercy of the kidnappers.

Again, equipment was rolled up. His lower leg was brushed with a pleasantly warm paste. The moment he realized what that might be, he already felt the intense, brief pain that came when the wax together with his leg hair was torn off.

Apparently now everything was done, which he had previously refused to do. The tormentors worked their way up his entire body. Except for the pubic hair, they did not leave out a square centimeter of skin from his neck down. He had no sense of how long the tournament lasted. Due to the many changes in the bondage, everything lasted even longer. At some point, he found himself in his original position. Finally, they were done.

After that, he was left alone. He could hear that everyone had left the room. They had kindly freed him from the gag, after he had nodded to the question "Be quiet now?"

***

Yvonne had a nice day, as recommended. She had told the receptionist that her husband would probably not come back because he had to drive to the north on business. Whether they believed her or not, she did not care. She decided to start with a guided city tour.

***

After some time, MM got another visit from his kidnappers. They started to open his blindfold.

"Keep close!"

MM nodded. He was sure that he did not wanted to know what the kidnappers looked like. By now, he had not the slightest chance of finding them with an identikit picture or that kind. But as soon as he saw the faces, he could identify them and they ran the risk of being found if they eventually released him. He was sure, that his life was rather save as long as he didn't see them.

They took off the bandage and immediately pressed a kind of bandage on his eyes, which they fixed with a large plaster. So again, he had the security not to accidentally look at the kidnappers. As he had expected, a hairdresser seemed to be working on him now. Surely, he would now dye him the previously requested green hair. In fact, his hair was soon covered with a paste that remained inside for a long time until it was rinsed out again. From the sounds he could imagine that the result was as expected. Then his hair was cut and even shaved in the neck. MM had no idea what kind of hairstyle, if this was the correct word, was created.

Next, work was done on his face. Apparently, something was applied. Again, he had no idea what that could be.

He was then – still naked - released from the chair. His hope that he would get some food was disappointed when he realized he had been taken back to bed. This time he was put on his stomach and fixed again on all four corners. The eyes were covered with the old bandage again. He had to confess that he endured all day without the slightest chance of an outbreak.

***

Yvonne let the evening end at the hotel bar. After she made it clear to some gentlemen that she was not looking for company, she was finally left alone and enjoyed it to the fullest.

Sunday 15th May

The flight would be in the evening. She still had enough time to do another little city tour. Her thoughts revolved around MM. What did the blackmailer do with him? Would he present himself? No, probably not, because if he knew MM even a little bit, he would know that MM would not hesitate to destroy his existence.

Presumably, the blackmailer would not personally appear, but use any assistants. Finally, he had more than enough money from the burglary. The only question was what he wanted to do with MM or to MM.

***

A few miles away, MM could have answered this question well. After he had been led to the toilet as the day before and had gotten something to drink, he expected to be fixed at this dental chair again. But now he was tied while standing. He suspected that he was in a sort of frame with many eyelets that would make it easy for his abductors to fasten his shackles at just the appropriate height. MM quickly realized that it was time to get dressed. First, he was put in pants that reminded him of Luxembourg. What else could he have expected? They would force him back into that ugly latex. When the pants were completely pulled up, he noticed that the pants seemed to have feet. The waistband of pants went to his belly button. Apparently, they tied a belt on him. He wondered why it smelled so strongly of rubber. Probably the pants had just been taken out of their pack. That had to be the reason. He knew that. Like a new inflatable mat. It stank pitifully of rubber at the beginning.

The next item were fingerless gloves that went under his armpits. The gloves were also closed with a belt at their ends. Instead of the expected shirt he now had to put on boots. As expected, of course, they had high heels. After the zippers were closed, the kidnappers were still working on them for a while. MM had no idea what they were doing, but was smart enough to keep his legs still and ask no questions. Finally, a shirt was slipped over him. It seemed to have short sleeves, which apparently also had their own closure. As a result, MM was not surprised when again a belt was tied on him. And again, it needed some extra time.

When he was finished, he was left standing for a while before being led out of the room. He noticed from the draft that they left the house and walked across a kind of square. A little later he was back in the minivan which immediately started. When they stopped, he heard many voices. Apparently, there were a lot of people who were busy walking back and forth. Some place in the city? He would have liked to attract attention. Maybe this was his only chance for the next days. But the kidnappers had gagged him as a precaution. He just did not know what was going to happen.

He himself would probably be noticed like a colored dog. So, he just had to get noticed in the public. For sure his kidnappers were aware of that. They would never offer a chance.

But then something happened that he would have never dreamed of. The kidnappers helped him out of the car, loosened his handcuffs, got back in the car, and drove away. When MM realized that he had been released, he undid his blindfold and found himself surrounded by many tourists in front of the departure terminal of the airport. This also made him realize why one of the kidnappers had whispered "gate 5" in his ear.

When MM looked at himself, he realized that the whole outfit was froggy green. In addition, the shirt had, as expected, short sleeves, but he had not guessed that it had puffy sleeves and that it ran down in a skirt. So, in fact it was a dress.

***

The check-in would close in half an hour. Yvonne had, as proposed by the blackmailer, the papers of MM with her. The only thing missing was MM. At the other end of the hall, a larger group of tourists seemed to have arrived again. A crowd of laughing people moved slowly in her direction. She wondered what she should do if MM did not arrive early enough. She would have no choice but to check in again at the hotel. But at least tomorrow she would have to contact the police. The tourists came closer and closer. They all seemed to be fixed to a point in the middle of the group. Maybe they had discovered a pop star or something similar. When Yvonne saw that some of the people were holding up cameras and mobile phones to shoot photos, she remembered the Japanese from Luxembourg.

She looked closer and could make out a frog-green figure around which the tourists had grouped. When they were only a few meters away, the idea became certainty. MM made it in time.

Her concern switched to gloating. This was the price he had to pay for constantly refusing the blackmailers demands. She decided to treat him as if his performance was the most normal thing in the world.

„Hi MM, here you are at last."

She gave him a kiss on the cheek.

„We have to check in quickly, otherwise we'll stay here longer."

It seemed to have gone to great lengths to make MM look convincing. She would have enough time on the plane to take a closer look. MM was visibly relieved to see her. After her welcome, however, his blood pressure still seemed to rise. She decided to give him the tip that Beatrice had given her a few days earlier.

„Listen, MM. Act as if you often run around like this. You've just gotten away from an event with friends too late, so you did not have time to change. Just try to give the impression that your outfit is something completely normal. At least for you."

Meanwhile, they were already at the counter and Yvonne presented her documents with businesslike face. The woman behind the counter, to Yvonne's delight, did her best to look completely uninvolved, but could not really keep her eyes off

MM. Surprisingly, he still did not make a sound, although he got all these looks. Yvonne was looking forward to the moment, when he would let his anger out. She was just curious whom he would choose as a victim.

At customs, it was embarrassing for MM again. When the officer saw him, he called into the room behind him „Olhe para os temos de!"

Yvonne did not know what that meant, but could quickly figure it out as the officer's colleagues immediately joined him and joked about MM.

„What is the problem?"

Yvonne had not expected this remark from MM. He had actually taken her advice to heart. For the officials, however, it was a reason to break into uncontrollable laughter. Yvonne did not know where that could have led to. But another officer had been attracted by the laughter. Apparently, that was the supervisor, because after a few words in command tone, everyone moved to their jobs.

„I'm so sorry. They are like little kids" the officer tried to apologize to MM and Yvonne. „Please come here."

He pointed to the control system for metallic objects. A short time later, they were through and could directly walk through the already opened gangway. Yvonne finally had time to take a closer look at MM. The red complexion was gone. What she had not recognized immediately in the rush, were red ornamental lines that covered his entire face. MM stared straight ahead into the back seat in front. Yvonne was not sure if he knew about the henna tattoo on his face. To avoid unnecessary riot, she decided not to point it out. Before she could continue her closer look, MM had awakened to activity.

„Put off these silly rings!"

He started fumbling around with his ear. Green fingernails were certainly a new experience for him.

„If you take your pretty fingers away, I want to see what I can do."

He looked first at her and then at his fingers.

„Oh God. Wait until I get hold on him!"

„Don't make a big show now. After all, you have to endure a few hours in these things. Or do you think, I have spare clothes in my hand luggage?"

He looked directly at her.

„Where have you been? What did you do to save me?"

Yvonne did not even try to get at his earrings.

„I did not do anything. What do you think? Do you think I'm some kind of superhero who always knows exactly where the bad guys are? How could I possibly know what happened to you?"

„Ever heard of the police?"

MM tapped her forehead with his fingers.

„Is there anything in there that resembles a brain?"

Yvonne wiped off his fingers with an angry gesture.

„No problem. Next time you want to live out your rubber fetish, I'll report a missing person."

She waved her fingers at quotation marks.

„My husband is being blackmailed because he has done tons of illegal business. Now I'm afraid that the blackmailer kidnapped him. But do not tell him that I said that about the illegal business."

MM was obviously fighting for self-control.

„Of course, I meant that you could come up with an appropriate story and then submit a search report."

„You would have had to look for another wife for that. I already refuted all the stories that came to mind before I even finished them. If someone has messed up things, it's still you and no one else."

If he had known how much his face paint undermined his authority, he probably would have liked to lock himself in the toilet. Anyway, Yvonne noticed that it was fun to irritate him with her arguments. She felt like a strong tree being attacked by a gentle breeze that was a mighty storm a long time ago.

„What do you imagine Yvonne? You have lived wonderfully from my money, right? And now suddenly there are problems, and of course, I'm all to blame!"

„You could answer that if you'd first of all would have told me about your business earlier. Much earlier. And secondly, if you were able to take my help on the current issues. But no, that's not the way big MM does it. MM always knows what to do. But now it looks like you have found your master. He has shown you some tricks, doesn't he?"

She ran her hand through his green hair.

„Pretty bob. With a shaved neck. Courageous."

MM touched his head and tried to figure out on what length his hair was left. Yvonne rummaged in her purse.

„Here you are."

She handed him her makeup mirror.

MM stared in disbelief at the henna tattoo. He tried to wipe away the lines. Even the fingers moistened with spit brought no success.

„What's this? I can't get it away. Yvonne do something!"

„Psss. Chill out. This looks like a henna tattoo. Nothing bad. That will fade with the time."

„Well. I have to return to the office tomorrow."

„Well, not so fast actually. I think it will be a fortnight." Yvonne explained in an unconcerned tone.

„What? Are you crazy?"

MM had given up all restraint.

„Now calm down. You do not want to entertain the whole plane?"

In fact, individual passengers kept coming to catch a glimpse of MM.

„The hair also takes some time to regrow"

„I can still cut off or dye with a different color" MM tried to explain. „But my face. Nothing works? Why does it take so long?"

„If I'm right, henna penetrates to the top skin layer, which is completely renewed on average about every 14 days. That is, when the red skin falls off, the color is gone. That's how it works."

„There must be an antidote."

„Not that I know, but you can ask in a beauty salon or the dermatologist" Yvonne suggested. Her MM in a beauty salon. That could have been one of the blackmailer's jobs.

„You'll check it out on the internet tomorrow. And I want to hear that it works! Did I make myself clear?"

„Yes Massa."

„Good and now take those stupid rings out of my ear!"

MM did not seem to be confused by her answer. Nevertheless, Yvonne finally decided to take a closer look at the rings in his ear. It suited her anger on MM well that she found her guess confirmed.

„They look pretty endless" she told him.

„Are you kidding? Do you think the ear has grown around it?"

„Would you like to drink something?"

The friendly stewardess had arrived.

"No", was MMs refusal. Yvonne asked for a water.

„What do you mean by endless?"

„Endless. I can't find a closure. I once read that there are such rings, which are made in a way that the closure is barely recognizable. Opening is not provided for this variety."

MM looked at her blankly.

„Does that mean that I have to keep them now until my life ends?"

„No, but you will probably need pliers or better a bolt cutter."

Smiling, she added: „When did you let them do it you?"

MM managed to gnash his teeth while answering.

„I did not let it do. It was just done to me without asking. You're really such a stupid cow."

Yvonne lay back in her chair waiting for his next question that came rather quick.

"Why do you want to know that?"

„The material is quite thick. Normally, only the area of the ring that sticks out of the ear is thick and the part in the flesh

91

is tiny. But your rings are constantly thick. So, the holes are larger than normal ear holes. But no matter, at the moment it looks like you have to keep them until tomorrow."

In MMs eyes the shock was obvious.

„It's just because of the size of the hole a bit stupid."

Yvonne got more and more fun.

„I do not know if they will close again."

MM pointed to his nose

„What about this?"

Yvonne took a closer look at the ring. She resisted the stimulus for better investigation to stick her little finger through the ring. Instead, she said „Ergo" with a regretful sigh.

„Ergo? What ergo? What does that mean? Do you need to use foreign words that you do not even know?"

„Ergo is just another word for:" Yvonne pronounced each word very clearly. „The same."

„What I say. You better not use foreign words. 'Ditto' is the word. From now on please in mother tongue!"

„Then ditto."

She rolled her eyes annoyed.

„Anyway, you can't open it."

MM started fumbling with the zipper of his boots.

„What are you doing?" Yvonne wanted to know.

„What do you think what it looks like? I open these boots. In Germany, I can probably go without it?"

„Yeah. I'm just wondering why you do not simply pull it down. That's not so difficult"

Meanwhile, he pulled with all his strength on the zipper.

„Those motherfuckers cut this ... this thing to pull down."

„Zipper is the word MM."

To be on the safe side, she repeated the word again slowly.

„But I do not know if I'm allowed to use that word. It could possibly be of foreign origin. Presumably, 'thing' is really the better term."

„Yes, then just the zipper. And now finally stop with your stupid bitchy acting."

He finally put his leg down on his knee to take a closer look at the zipper.

„Wow, MM. That's at least 5 inches."

She stroked the chunky heels.

„Respect. Not everyone dares to do that."

The brain-remark and the 'stupid cow' from earlier did not want to get out of her head. What did this little wannabe center of the universe actually presumed to do? Did he really think he was the only one who consumed wisdom with spoons? And now this super-intelligent creature was sitting next to her and failed at a simple zipper.

„Now look at this. They have closed the whole zipper with superglue. Do you have a pair of scissors?"

She stroked his smooth thighs and cooed, „sure my love. Only it is not in hand luggage. We are sitting in a plane. You can't have that in your hand luggage. Didn't you know that?"

„Stop it with your sarcasm. I am in an emergency situation here. Even I sometimes can forget such details."

He pushed her hand away.

„And stop stroking my legs like that. Just open the zipper. Maybe you are at least capable of doing so!"

Yvonne leaned back in her chair and crossed her arms.

„You have to solve some task yourself. You still have enough time. The flight takes another two hours."

„Then at least help me to remove this wide belt. It is far too tight."

„This is a waist belt my love. It has to sit that tight. It is created for that."

She closed her eyes. If she could fall asleep now, he would certainly go crazy.

„I do not care about the name. I want to take that off anyway."

He groped and tugged at the belt without finding a fastener. Yvonne watched his actions for a while.

„If I look at it closely, one could already call that a corset. A small one. I'm not sure."

She put her index finger to her forehead to emphasize her thought process and carried out small massage movements. MM glared at her.

„I do not give a shit what it is called! I want to take that off!"

„Could you please be more considerate, sir?"

The friendly stewardess was back. As Yvonne looked up to her, she realized that MM still had the full attention of all passengers.

„You can see that I have a problem. So, let me search for a solution."

Wonderful thought Yvonne, now start an argument with the stewardess.

„You have a somewhat unconventional clothing, sir. This is by no means a problem for me. If it's a problem for you then you would have had to opt for another wardrobe before departure."

MM stared at the stewardess with his eyes wide open. Unaffected, the stewardess continued

„My problem is that for the other passengers you make an undisturbed flight impossible. Should you continue this, we will have to have an intermediate landing to your expense and, to our great regret, have to hand you over to the authorities."

Without waiting for an answer, she turned away and headed for the galley. Yvonne thought she had observed an uncontrollable twitching of her mouth. The stewardess seemed to fight down a laugh.

„What do I have to do now?" MM whispered „how does it work?"

„Normally, a corset has front metal closures and a lacing at the back" she whispered back. „However, you're wearing a model that does not have these closures because there's a covering decorated with stylish ornaments above it."

She indicated the covering.

„Normally you would expect a Velcro or kind of hocks under it. Here, however, is nothing to find. It seems to me that again a large amount of glue was used."

Again, Yvonne leaned back comfortably in her chair.

„What does that mean?" his whisper had almost become a scream.

„Since I still do not have any scissors, you will have to wear this pretty garment for a while."

Yvonne had no problem with continuing to whisper.

„You simply do not want to help. I can't believe you can't open any of those disgusting clothes."

His voice was back to the old volume.

„Sir. Let me introduce myself. My name is Paul. I am the copilot. You were already requested by the stewardess to behave a little more inconspicuously. I would also like to ask you to lower your conversation to an appropriate volume."

He addressed Yvonne directly.

„Would you prefer to take another seat to enjoy the rest of the flight in peace?"

Yvonne was enthusiastic about that offer.

She met MM at the luggage belt again.

„Would you like to go to the parking garage right away or should I get the car and you wait here?"

MM did not seem to have dealt with that idea.

„You want to drive? The Bentley? You never did it before."

Yvonne smiled at him.

„Because that never occurred to you. But now", she pointed to his boots, „the question arises how much practice you already have with these heels. Maybe driving is still a bit too early?"

They once again became the focus of the fellow traveler's interest. Knowing this, MM tried to speak quietly.

„We go to the parking garage together. Afterwards you're not able to find me again or you make a scratch in my car, because you're acting too stupid when parking. I'm the first choice for this job."

„We can also take a taxi", suggested Yvonne clearly audible.

„Then you can pick up the car tomorrow if you've swapped

this wonderful outfit for your boring everyday clothes again. What do you think?"

MM grabbed the last suitcase they had been waiting for.

„We're going to the parking garage now and that's it."

„OK. You can also sit on the trolley with the suitcases if walking becomes too difficult."

„Now finally shut your face. You're such a bitch. I do not want to hear anything anymore."

Yvonne pursed her lips tightly and nodded well-behaved. She took the trolley and left with a brisk pace. MM did his best to keep up with her. To her astonishment, he did indeed succeed. Arriving at the car, she decided to praise him for it.

„You already have a very good walk. Did they practice in Portugal with you?"

MM packed the suitcases in the car, got the keys and drove off. Yvonne stayed behind in the parking deck. When she arrived at the exit after some time, MM was standing at the closed barrier. She held the ticket up.

„Looking for that?"

„All right then. Hop in!"

She walked to the passenger side, which was decorated with a long scratch. She decided to ask him later. Presumably he had taken a turn too tight in the parking garage.

When they finally got home, it took several hours to cut MM out of all things. He fell into the bed and was asleep in the same moment. On his back, also indicated as a henna tattoo, she saw an Internet address. The blackmailer seemed to get a likeable person.

Monday 16th May

„Morning Yvonne. You have to remove the color out of my face today. Can I dye my hair with an appropriate color or am I cutting it off?"

MM had, as always, put on a white shirt and tie. With the green bob and the ornaments on the face that wasn't a convincing look. Yesterday she had liked him much better.

„This night, I surfed the internet for a while."

„Very good Yvonne. So, go ahead."

„I wasn't curious about the henna. I already told you that you can't wash henna. But after all, that will fad rather soon. You can barely see it in about 1 to 2 weeks. Be glad the guy did not really tattoo you. But as I said that was not my concern. I was on a website the blackmailer wrote on your back."

„My back?" MM tried to look at his back, but stopped the attempt immediately, because he could not see through the shirt anyway. Yvonne was sure he would not have seen anything bare-chested. He wasn't that flexible.

„And? What is there again?"

„It's best to have a look yourself. But first you drink a coffee."

She pushed the coffee towards him. Not caring about the slopped over puddle, MM took the coffee cup and went to the laptop.

„I see nothing. All black."

„You just have to move the mouse. I left the page open."

She could watch wonderfully from the breakfast table, how MMs face once again went through all colors between lime white and scarlet red.

„Yvonne. Can you put some skin-colored make-up on my face so that I can go among people without attracting attention like a freak?"

„Sure, I only have to get it first. I know the right shop in the city. By the way, I believe 'colorful dog' would be a better fitting comparison than freak", Yvonne laughed.

„I can't find anything funny about it. I have to ask you to be much more constructive. Is that clear? Already yesterday in the plane you got on my nerves!"

The volume of his voice had increased more and more. He tried to calm down a bit again.

„And if you have to go shopping, bring an electric shaver right away to cut off my hair. Everything else takes too long."

He pointed in the direction of the door.

„Get started. I have to work here first. But in two hours at the latest, I want to be through the door."

„Yes Massa. Your faithful servant is already on the way."

She was not sure if he had heard her answer yet. She had to time that better in the future.

When she returned with her purchases, MM was on the phone. Although he was sitting in another room, he could hardly be missed.

„I do not care what the guy put on the net about you. You get a lot of wages and I expect perfect work. From now on you work the list off and if you work 24/7. I expect successes. Tomorrow at this time, I want to hear that you are much further. And goodbye."

Before Yvonne could imagine, what he would have done with the phone receiver if it would have been such an old one, he was already in front of her.

„Did you get everything. I have an urgent appointment"

Without waiting for an answer, he sat down at the table and waited for his facial treatment.

„I would suggest to shave off your hair first. Otherwise the hair may stick to your make-up. How did you take your piercings out?"

„Of course, with the bolt cutter."

He was visibly happy that he got rid of the jewelry. The only question was how the blackmailer would think about it, as he had announced on the website that in the future MM would always run around with the piercings done in Lisbon.

„You've read that the guy with your papers has a different opinion?"

„Listen closely Yvonne. I'll try to explain this for the last time. In the hope that even you understand it: I do not let this sick brain dictate what I have to wear and how I should look. Did you understand that now?"

Yvonne handed him the razor.

„Then get started. I'll see if we got new mails."

She could easily hear him from her room. He explained the mirror what he would do in the moment the blackmailer was in his hands. Meanwhile, she read the new mail from the blackmailer.

„Beloved friends, as I could see, you have already looked at the small website. Yvonne, you can only guess. But MM, you simply know it. The information I present to the interested visitors is only a small part of the material in my possession.

In the meantime, hopefully you will have recovered a bit from the exciting trip to Lisbon. Would be important, because true to the principle 'A rolling stone gathers no moss', I have already prepared another trip. In order not to overstain you Yvonne, you may also like to skip this journey. However, I would like to see MM at the destination. I can't promise, but maybe, dear MM, we'll get to know each other personally.

Presumably, you'll have already taken all sorts of efforts to get rid of your eye-catching hair and your exciting face painting. That's okay. However, I would like to express the hope that you did not decided to remove your piercings.

Now to the little puzzle that needs to be solved.

The next trip takes you, dear MM, back to a European capital. This time, it is only the second largest in the country. There you will visit the "Castrum Puellarum". Take a hotel for five days. If you want to come along Yvonne, all you need is a camera and some good books. I am afraid, you can't accompany MM on his appointments.

Departure is on Wednesday, the day after tomorrow. So take a break and enjoy.

Please be so kind to give me a quick reply to this email. I am particularly interested in the information which hotel you choose. Since I do not want to rely on communicating with MM by Internet, this information would be very helpful to me. MM is a bit awkward in these things."

„Again, a problem solved."

MM came bumping into the room with a bald head.

„Now the make-up and I can finally set off"

Yvonne barely looked up at him.

„You really have to hurry up with your activities. You have already received the next invitation for a city tour."

Yvonne pointed to the screen.

„Well, the man shows his first weakness. When I get to know him, that's synonymous with his final defeat."

MM rubbed his hands and picked up the phone and dialed a number.

„Where are we travelling to?"

He looked questioningly at Yonne. Before she could answer, his interlocutor answered.

„Watch out. We have the big breakthrough ahead of us. The blackmailer has contacted again. This time he wants to meet me."

MM put his hand over the phone and looked at Yvonne.

„What destination?"

When she shrugged, he told her to find the place and then tell him in the next few minutes. Then he left the room.

„I already told you this morning that I'm not interested in your objections. We will finally create facts ..."

Yvonne did not get any more.

She turned to the Internet with a sigh. The input 'Castrum Puellarum' immediately led her to Edinburgh. A second check showed her that Glasgow was indeed bigger than Edinburgh. She turned toward the door and screamed as loud as she could „Edinburgh".

Immediately came as thanks „That was about time. Book a room for me."

„Yes Massa, then go ahead. Meet your ruin. As though the blackmailer is so stupid and meet you at the hotel bar for a little chat."

She booked a single room at the Holiday Inn, gave the information to the blackmailer, and shut down the computer.

MM stood in the bathroom in front of the mirror and creamed his face with concealer. It actually worked. The look was a bit unnatural, but the lines of the tattoo were covered and MM was finally able to leave the house. Yvonne refrained from making him aware that he had spread the concealer on his new white-colored bald head very incompletely.

„It's getting very late today. I have a lot to do. Do not wait for me with dinner."

With that he was gone. After two hours she had the house back in shape and headed, dressed with her corset, in the city. She hoped she could reduce her MM-frustration at Beatrice shop. She soon needed to know whether she was ready to endure MMs shameless behavior until the blackmail ended, or if she had to worry about making a fundamental cut in her life right now. Even if the blackmailer was eventually identified, she wondered if she wanted to stay with MM. She had learned to much about him in the past three weeks. Even though he might then be the caring MM again.

After spending some time in the city, she went to Beatrice.

„You are looking good. You had a good time in Lisbon?"

Beatrice immediately blurted out the question that Yvonne really wanted to avoid.

„Was nothing special", she tried to finish that topic. On the other hand, she was still so mad at MM that a little more information for Beatrice could not hurt either.

„No, that's not right. The visit was a complete disaster for my husband. He has been in the grip of some freaks for a couple of days doing some stuff with him that he did not like."

Beatrice took Yvonne by the arm.

„If you want, you can tell me about it while you're changing clothes."

When Yvonne started putting on her usual outfit, she talked about the transformation that MM had been through.

„Wow." Beatrice was impressed. „And then you wanted to tell me first, nothing special had happened? What did the police say about that?"

„Police was no option. He was so embarrassed that he wanted to avoid further excitement."

Actually, that was not even a real lie. Yvonne had just left out the essential reason.

„To put it straight to the point Yvonne. Might your husband have a penchant for such fetish things? I mean, a lot of people just leave the guts at the crucial moment and then they're lying about gangsters and raids."

Yvonne could not help laughing.

„No definitely not. Everyone, but MM. He definitely made it involuntary."

„You call your husband MM? Does he like champagne?"

„Our German champagne? No, that's another story."

„Okay, so he did that involuntarily. Have you already searched the web for the video?"

„Video?" Yvonne had not thought of that yet. „Do you think they filmed it?"

„Of course, we do not live in the Stone Age anymore."

Beatrice went into the office and motioned for Yvonne to follow her.

„There are various sides of crazy fetish people. If there is a video, then we will find it quickly. What did the latex clothes look like?"

„Everything was greenish. He had tight pants, platform boots, a dress with puffed sleeves and long gloves. That's it. All in all. "

After looking for a while, Beatrice actually found it. Under the headline „Latex makeover" she found the piercings and the big show at the airport as a video.

„From what it looks like, he really does not seem to have done that voluntarily."

„I wonder why I did not get it myself. It's clear that such guys hold a camera when they do that."

Beatrice looked questioningly at Yvonne for a while.

„I think there's a lot more going on. But it's okay if you do not want to tell me. After all, we only known each other for a few days."

„You're right. There is much more."

Yvonne finally told Beatrice the whole story.

„Wow. I have to say. Your MM is in deep shit." She put her hand over her mouth „Ups. I meant of course that he is in a tight spot."

„Yes. You're right. Whether you believe it or not, he has a completely different view on it. He believes every day that he is close to a breakthrough. Today he got a new mail, which ordered him to Edinburgh. The kidnapper suggested that they might meat. MM takes it as a commitment. He will fly there because he thinks he'll get him now."

„And what about you?"

„The blackmailer has basically released me. I should only fly if I want."

„And?"

„You do not know MM. He immediately decided that I did not want to. To be honest, I really do not feel like flying with him. MM decides everything anyway. He has no interest in listening to my advice."

Beatrice looked at her watch.

„You have to get started."

She reached into a box and pulled out wristbands and ankle bands, made of stainless steel similar to her collar.

„We said that you had to make amends for the two days you were in Lisbon", she told her as she put the jewelry on her.

„So, you do not have to clean for too long, I've decided to expand your work outfit a little."

She attached a chain to one of the wristbands, pulled it through the ring on the collar, and then slid another lock into the other wristband. If Yvonne now wanted to stretch one arm very far, she automatically pulled the other towards her neck.

„I have chosen a long chain, so you are not too limited."

Before the surprised Yvonne could answer back, Beatrice had already pulled her into the sales room and pressed the cleaning utensils into her hands.

„If you get the idea to argue now, I'll put a gag in your mouth", she whispered in her ear before she disappeared into another part of the store.

„What do you think? Shall we meet again this evening?"

Yvonne had already changed and sat in the back room at a cozy chat with Beatrice. To her own astonishment, she was by no means angry with Beatrice about the sales promotion with the chain. On the contrary, she considered it a welcome challenge to do a good job despite the constraints.

„Okay, why not? Is there a pub or restaurant nearby where we can meet?"

„Yes, but you can pick me up here as well and you'll bring me to my home. My friend can cook something for us. Then we talk again."

Beatrice looked expectantly at Yvonne. After a moment's hesitation, she finally agreed.

Unlike Yvonne had expected, Beatrice did not live in a rented flat, but in a small family home in a quiet residential area. It was not hard for Beatrice to guess Yvonne's thoughts.

„Before you get the idea that my shop or the job of my friend throws off so much. My parents gave it to me a long time ago. Kind of heritage."

„Super. If you live more or less for free, that makes things easier."

By then they had arrived at the house and could hear that someone was busy in the kitchen.

„Come in, I'll be ready soon."

In the kitchen stood a 2-meter man, who welcomed her with a friendly laugh.

„Hello, I'm Rondo and you can only be Yvonne."

He pointed to the big kitchen table.

„Sit down, the salad is already waiting for you."

During the meal, they talked about all the world and his wife. Only when the table was cleared, Beatrice brought the conversation back to MM.

„Rondo has a lot of experience in research. He is a freelance journalist. This is a job that leaves him a lot of freedom."

The two laughed at each other.

„Insider joke?" Yvonne wanted to know.

„Yes, but too complicated to explain. Sorry."

„Beatrice already told me about your husband on the phone. I was so free to roam the nct a bit."

Rondo was now the concentrated investigator.

„My suggestion is that we fly undercover to Edinburgh at our own expense and try to figure out what's going on there with your husband."

Yvonne looked at Beatrice.

„Do you think that you shouldn't have asked me first, before you tell everything to Rondo?"

Beatrice put her hand on Yvonne's arm.

„Sorry, but the thought came to me when you were already gone. Since I don't have your number, I decided so. I thought that you would agree."

„I would have. But since MM always decides everything for me and I do not want to continue in that way."

She rummaged in her purse and finally pulled out a business card

„Here you are. Landline and mobile."

„Sorry again, that wasn't correct."

„Okay. We do not have to dramatize that now either."

Yvonne turned back to Rondo.

„How do you want to do that? As far as I know, monitoring people is only easy at the cinema screen. In real life you certainly need a well-rehearsed and sufficiently large team."

„In principle, you are right. If we do that in a threesome, we really run the risk of being left emptyhanded at the end of the action, but it can work."

Yvonne leaned back. "Tell us."

„So, if I understood correctly, MM is a complete failure on the computer. Therefore, the kidnapper in Edinburgh does not want to contact him via the network. Of course, this limits his options greatly, as he now has to make contact himself or he needs somebody to act as middleman."

„But he can also simply leave an information at the reception. After all, he knows where MM resides." Yvonne interjected.

„Right. In this way, he himself remains wonderfully out of the game. The question is what the message can be."

„Definitely not: we meet at 8pm at the hotel bar. You recognize me by the green jacket with the blue rose in the buttonhole"

Beatrice began to chuckle. „No, rather: Come completely in latex, then I'll recognize you."

„Now stay serious. After all, we want to talk about a very difficult action here in a very short time."

Rondo was still the organizer.

„My guess is he'll see to it that MM leaves the hotel. He'll probably send him somewhere by taxi."

„And then we drive with another taxi afterwards. 'Follow this car there'" Beatrice continued the story. Rondo looked at her with depressed expression on his face.

„That's not how it works, Beatrice. I do not have to get the gag from our playroom now?"

„No isn't necessary" Beatrice laughed at him relaxed. „I will be serious from now on."

Yvonne looked a bit confused between the two.

„Don't pretend to be surprised Yvonne." Beatrice pointed to her feet. „You know that I sometimes wear locks on my boots. Surely you can't be surprised if we have a small playroom here."

Yvonne hoped she would not blush now.

„No, I could have imagined that."

Beatrice took Yvonne by the hand.

„Come on, you're ready for a guided tour."

Without further questions, she opened the door to their playroom.

„Here, of course, we have some nice bondage items. This collar, for example. Something similar to the one you wear while you work in my shop."

Without further questioning, she put the collar around Yvonne's neck.

„Only this band is much wider. As you sure recognized, you are now a little restricted in your freedom of movement."

„You don't want to let me wear everything you have here, right?"

„No of course not. But the collar looks amazingly good on you. Have a look in the mirror."

Yvonne felt like a proud princess with her head held high in front of her people.

„Yes, you are right. This has something very special. Only I believe that in the long run it will be quite annoying."

„Just try it. We have a lot to discuss."

„Time does not stop for us", Rondo admonished them as they returned to the kitchen. „I see you try one of the collars? I hope that's not the one with the special lock."

„Very funny. You're kidding, don't you?" Yvonne wasn't sure.

„We'll find a way", was the reassuring answer from Beatrice.

„Let's move on. We were at the chase. Of course, we do not do this by taxi, but by rental car. It's best if each of us has one. Then we are prepared for all cases. We keep in contact with each other via mobile phone."

„Wait, sorry, that's MM" Yvonne picked up her cell phone and walked out of the room. „What's up?"

When she came back, her expression had changed.

„What happened Yvonne?" Beatrice wanted to know. „You look like he's scared the hell out of you."

„You could say so." She sat down. „MM is on the run. He has received information from his private snoop that the police is on his trail and wants to arrest him for a murder he did not commit."

Rondo and Beatrice stared at each other.

„Okay. No chase in Edinburgh."

Yvonne did not seem to listen.

„He also said that our villa is under surveillance. If I did not want to conduct a long interview with the police, I'd better sleep elsewhere."

„Of course, you can stay with us first."

„And I'm not supposed to call him anymore, because he would throw his phone in the trash now. He would contact me, when the time has come."

Yvonne raised her eyes and looked at them

„What should I do now?"

Beatrice took her hand.

„You stay here for now. Tomorrow we will see. But you can explain one thing right now. Why are you so depressed? Not too long ago, you were angry of MM."

After a moment of hesitation Yvonne smiled at Beatrice.

„Right. Probably that's just the difference between 'being unhappy but knowing what the next day will bring' and 'happy but not knowing what the next day will bring'. That's all."

„If that is your whole concern then I am confident that we will fill the next day with lots of interesting things."

***

Meanwhile, MM was curled up in the trunk of Karlsson's car. Not half an hour before, Karlsson had showed up in MMs office and told him that he had been on the case the whole time and had played the 'turning tail' number only for possible wiretaps. He had looked at MM, as if actually no further explanation would be necessary. MM, who was completely surprised, did not want to compromise himself and took the explanation without further ado. Then Karlsson showed him a

108

car outside the door. Apparently, police officers in plain clothes were sitting in it. To reinforce the suspicion, he also showed him a small video that he had taken with his cell phone. MM could clearly see that exactly the car, which now stood in front of the door, had followed him through half the city. When Karlsson then explained that he had been told by a reliable source that MM was about to be arrested, MM was almost relieved when Karlsson explained the plan with the trunk.

They've been driving around for a while now and MM did not know if he had to vomit in the near future or not. Finally, Karlsson stopped and MM could hear him approaching the trunk.

They were on a quiet street in some forest. Karlsson handed him a key.

„Walk in that direction. After about one kilometer you will find a hunting lodge. Stay there until I can contact you. The owner is on holiday at the Canary Islands and will be back in two weeks."

Before MM could hold him back, he was already driving away with screeching tires. MM looked around helplessly. It was already dawning and he did not have the faintest idea where he was. He had thrown away his cell phone on the advice of Karlsson. His wallet could not help him either. Money and check cards were useless. Despite his fortune, at the moment he had nothing more than the clothes on his back and the key to the hunting lodge. He walked uncertain in the direction indicated. He had no idea where this blackmail could lead to.

The partially dense underbrush made him more problems than he liked. After fifteen minutes his beloved suit trousers were hopelessly damaged. Luckily, he had not lost his direction. He hit a forest road just wide enough for a car. The road led him to the announced hut. All the windows were locked with wooden shutters, so he did not need to worry that he might have arrived at the wrong place. The key was perfect and a little later he was sitting in the only room. As if someone

109

had expected him to come, the fridge was filled with some long-lasting foods. He could easily endure for a few days.

Tuesday 17th May

Yvonne absent-mindedly fingered the ring of her collar.

„I'm sorry with the lock Yvonne." Beatrice looked at her apologetically. „I really did not know that we have a problem with this collar. How did you sleep?"

„Not bad at all. Why not, after all, as far as I know, there are at least two peoples on earth, where the women wear much larger collars."

„Two? I thought that's just a tribe somewhere in Africa."

„Somewhere in the Far East, too. I think they are called giraffe women."

„Allegedly, they should die immediately if the rings are removed. They certainly have far too little muscles in the neck area."

„They wouldn't. There are even some who live permanently without the jewelry. Only they look a bit strange because their clavicles are pushed down. Besides, these are not rings. This is a long tube wrapped around the neck. Rather a spiral."

„How do you know all this Yvonne?"

„Isn't that a general education? I think I saw that on one of these magazines on TV."

„Do you have any idea how to proceed?" Rondo intervened in the conversation.

„I think, I'll just return to the villa, live my normal life and wait and see what the day will bring. After all, nothing special can happen to me. If MM is guilty, then it is he who has something to fear. For me at most the questioning of the police is a bit annoying. But they'll get it someday that I can't help them."

„What about the blackmailer?"

„When he answers, I'll just tell him what happened and then I'll have a look at the things that will happen. So far, he did not have too much interest in my person."

„Okay", Rondo answered. „But if something happens, if we can help in any way, then ask Beatrice for assist. You're going to do the cleaning this afternoon anyway. Maybe then Beatrice will also get your collar unlocked. In the shop she has tons of spare keys. For the moment that does not bother you, right?"

„To be honest, not really. Has something exciting, if you do not know exactly, whether you ever get rid of the part again."

„Of course, if you see it that way, then I can attach much more to your body and throw away the keys." Beatrice offered.

„Don't bother. The collar is enough for the first time." Yvonne laughed.

As expected, Yvonne found no news from MM at the villa. But the blackmailer had reported again.

„Someone absconded. I'd say this is a mistake. If the good old MM should contact you somehow, please tell him that there are more tasks waiting for him. Very patient tasks. They can wait a whole year if necessary.

Have much fun with your new job. At least a start into the future."

Lately, so many things had happened that Yvonne did not think were possible, that she did not even wonder that the blackmailer knew about her cleaning job at Beatrice' shop. Speaking of cleaning. She changed into her latex outfit and started to make her clean house even cleaner.

***

At about the same time, MM was in the hunting lodge, desperately trying to get a clear idea of his situation. Looking at himself in the mirror in the morning, he could only feel aversion to what he saw. The make-up had disappeared and left those terrible lines in his face again. He still had the soiled shirt and partially torn suit from the day before. There were no clothes in the hut. If he ignored what had happened to him in Lisbon, he could not remember the last time he had put on some piece of clothing that he had been wearing the day before. And now he had to put on those stinking filthy things if he did not want to walk around completely naked. Why do hunting huts have no washing machines? The hunters are getting dirty too. At first, he had thought he could at least wash his things in the sink, but not a single drop would come out of the water tap.

Finally, he decided to explore the area. You never know what else could happen to you. There was no harm in having a certain knowledge of the area.

***

„We need to talk to Mr. Müller. I assume he is in the office?"

The blonde beauty at the reception pitifully raised her hands.

„MM, as we all call him, is absent. I can ask him to give a call back once he's at the office."

„When do you expect him?" Smidt had a sense of foreboding.

„I can't tell you unfortunately. I just received a short email this morning informing me that I should move all his meetings and dates." She pointed to the phone. „I've just finished the last."

„When did he send the mail?"

The young woman operated with the mouse for some seconds.

„The mail arrived yesterday evening at 5:35. So you can assume that he sent it less than a minute earlier."

„Who was still in the house at this time?"

Again, she did some clicks at the computer.

„You are lucky that I have access to the time recording system", she announced the two police officers joyfully.

„Here it is."

After a final mouse click, she smiled at them again.

„Nobody."

„So, he was alone in the company. I assume as a boss, his working time is not recorded?"

„You're right. He would only cheat himself after all. Makes no sense."

„Are there any other employees whose working hours are not recorded? Any executive employees?"

„No. If I may say so: MM puts great emphasis on control. He sometimes even requests a list of all his employees that should be present. Just to check it."

„And?"

A questioning look of the young woman.

„Does he always find all employees at the place, where they are supposed to be?" Smidt explained.

„You can bet your life on it! As soon as he asks for such a list, the information is distributed directly to all departments." She held her hand in front of her mouth in alarm. „Oh my God, if he finds out I have to find a new job."

„Then you should get a better control over your tongue."

Smidt put her card on the counter. „I expect that you inform me immediately if you know where to reach MM."

„You can rely on me."

Smidt raised her finger warningly.

„Not a single word about it to anyone. Not even to your best friends."

When the two police-officers had left the foyer, she picked up the phone.

„You do not believe what just happened ..."

„What do you think Rednich? Did he go into hiding?"

„Looks very much right now. I'm just not sure if Karlsson has anything to do with it. After all, he wasn't around MM that evening."

„Remember, we only know that his car was not near MMs car. We do not know anything about Karlsson himself. I suggest we visit MMs villa now. Maybe his wife knows something she wants to tell us."

„Why actually, MM should go into hiding?"

„Our investigation into the murder of Triebel? There is no evidence that suggests an urgent suspicion against him."

„None evidence we found by now" clarified Rednich.

„Exactly, that's what I mean. Of course, it does not have to be that way, but it would be at least plausible."

When they stopped in front of the villa, they already saw the car of MMs wife standing in the driveway.

„Women are always reliable." Smidt smiled at Rednich.

„Then I'm curious if she's cleaning again" Rednich replied.

She was cleaning. Only this time the two were not as surprised by her outfit as the first time, even if it was extended with a stainless-steel collar.

„May we come in shortly?" Smidt wanted to know.

Yvonne stepped aside.

„You already know the way. How can I help you?"

„With an information regarding your husband. We wanted to ask him a few more questions about the Triebel murder case, but can't reach him. That is very irritatingly."

Yvonne had settled on the front edge of a chair. She sat with her legs closed and very upright.

„My husband briefed me last night that he was going underground now. I should not worry because my bank-account is well stocked and, in some time, when the dust has settled and the police grabbed Triebel's murderer, he would come back to me."

She looked expectantly at the two of them.

In her career, Smidt had experienced a major part of lengthy witness interviews and was now somewhat surprised that Yvonne was so generous with her information.

„Do you have any idea where he might be?"

„No, I don't. And if I had an idea you would have no advantage from that. After all, my husband is not so stupid as to go to a place that I know, because he must realize that sooner or later you will come and ask me exactly that question."

„That's why I'm asking. You never know. Sometimes the strategy is to be exactly at that place where the police would never search because it is too obvious.

Yvonne smiled at Smidt.

„Well. Still, I do not know any place where I would look for him. But maybe you will find his car. He certainly will not leave it alone.”

„We have already found it.”

Yvonne raised her hands „well then…”

„So, I note that you have no idea where your husband might be?”

„It is exactly like that. He has no relationship I know. He does not have any friends I know. For a long time, his life takes place either in his company or here at home. Apart from that, he takes me out to dinner at least once a week and that's about it. So, you can see that I really can't help.”

After the two policemen said goodbye, Yvonne decided to tell them about blackmail on their next visit, if they finally asked sufficiently smart questions. She finished her house-cleaning quickly. After that, she had no time to change. So, she quickly put on a coat and made her way to Beatrice. After all, she did not want to jeopardize the only friendship that had fallen into her lap for a long time.

„Wow. You are on time and already in work clothes. Super Yvonne. What made you walk around in the public with such clothes?”

„First of all, I did not have time to change my clothes because the police disturbed me in the middle of my daily house-cleaning. And secondly, you can't see so much of the stuff again. I'm wearing a coat.”

„The coat covers little more than your butt. insofar …”

Yvonne looked at herself in the mirror and had to agree with Beatrice. Her outfit was really not quite the average. It also explained why she had the impression that she had drawn some glances as she walked the short distance from her car to the shop.

„No matter. Best I start right away?”

„Just a moment Yvonne. You haven't paid off your Lisbon-debt. At least not all.”

„The chain again?" Yvonne looked questioningly at Beatrice.

„Yep."

After Beatrice had put on the chain in the same way as the day before, she added without further explanation, a chain between the stainless-steel cuffs, which she had placed around her ankles.

„How is this supposed to work? That's too short!"

„If I would have chosen a longer one, you would just stumble on it. By the way, please remember: No discussion about your work clothes."

As always, they sat together in the small back room two hours later. Yvonne was freed from chains and cuffs.

„Have your sales of chains risen again?"

„Yes, they have. I can already tell you that you do not have to wear them tomorrow, because I have to wait for a new delivery first."

„But I was looking forward to it" Yvonne joked.

„No fear. The delivery will arrive no later than the day after tomorrow. So, you just have to last a day without it." With acted sympathy Beatrice put her hand on Yvonnes thigh "Will you be able to wait that long time?"

„I guess I have to. After all, I have no influence on my clothes. You kindly reminded me again."

„You really move very well when you clean my shop. Not many can do that. Almost as if the movement restriction would be really fun."

„To be honest. It is exactly like that. I would have never thought a few weeks ago that I find such clothes so stunning. And if someone had told me that I would enjoy cleaning a store like yours dressed like this, I would have sent him straight to the madhouse."

„I also have the impression that you found something unexpectedly exciting."

Yvonne sipped thoughtfully at her coffee

„Yes, who would have thought it?"

Beatrice looked at her watch.

„We are already late. I have to enter and sort the last delivery into the system. Take your time to drink your coffee. If we do not see each other again, see you tomorrow."

When Yvonne got into her car a little later, she noticed that Beatrice had forgotten to open her collar. She thought for a moment whether she should go back, but then drove off. Probably Beatrice had no time to search for the right key.

***

As MM returned from his exploration, he was happy to see Karlsson's car standing in front of the hut. Karlsson was still sitting in the car.

„Karlsson. Good that you're there. I urgently need..." MM did not finish. He saw the handle of a knife that stuck in Karlsson's chest. Right at the heart. Instinctively, MM grabbed the handle to pull out the knife, but found it unremovable.

There was no need for second thought. Karlsson was dead. Karlsson must have found something that would have brought MM forward in his problem. So Karlsson might have documents with him that MM absolutely had to have.

The moment he searched for the boot opener he heard a car coming through the forest. He had no choice but to get away from the hut as quickly as possible and watch what would happen from a safe distance. Shielded by the undergrowth, he ran bent down into the forest and finally crept behind a pile of wood.

A woman and a man got out of the car and approached Karlsson's car. The way they moved could only mean that they were police or professional killers. When the two discovered Karlsson, the man checked the pulse, while the woman's gaze scanned the surroundings and the hut, apparently to check whether there was danger. A few minutes later, the two had put away their weapons. There was already a siren in the distance.

MM moved away from the hut very carefully and then faster and faster. He did not know where to go. So, he just kept running straight ahead. In order not to coincidentally meet with hikers, he avoided every forest path he found. He had no idea how long he had run when he finally reached the edge of the woods and saw in front of him the foothills of his city, MM-City. He did not have a single idea what he should do now. He was not in a position to just let it go. Otherwise he could not pull the strings. No one to manipulate. A situation he never experienced before.

He tried to remember what Yvonne had told him. The henna-paintings on his face would have essentially disappeared in the next 14 days. As long as he looked like he did now, he could not show up in public. So, he had to survive the next two weeks in hiding. Actually, he had half a week behind him, since he had already received the painting on Saturday.

For the moment he could do nothing but stay in the forest away from the trails. Soon the first joggers would come. So, it was important to find a reasonable hiding place.

Apparently, a small party was taking place nearby in the forest. MM was able to identify increasingly loud music and the typical buzz that always arises when many people are chatting in one place. In fact, a little later he could make out a small clearing. Apparently young people had set up a proper camp. A team tent and various smaller tents all around, where they could sleep if they ever got around to do so. The only thing he missed was the cars with which the whole caboodle had been transported. MM circled around the camp at some distance until the tents gave way to a narrow, asphalted forest road. There stood the cars in a long row. A look at the camp showed him that the people were still busy with themselves. One group had the loud conversation he heard all the time. If these idiots ever had the idea to turn down the music, they could have saved their vocal cords. The kind of music he heard, however, was very different from what he expected. It consisted only of a series of uniform tones. Turned slightly quieter, the music would certainly have been suitable for meditation or the like. MM could only shake his head.

Under cover of the trees, he moved cautiously in the direction of the cars.

„Hello dear human! Take courage and join us. Do not be scared."

MM stopped in shock. He did not realize how he could have overlooked the man with long white hair, a white beard and a flowing robe. But now he had been caught and had to make the best of it. He turned completely to the man.

„I did not want to disturb your camp."

The man spread his arms in a way that made MM fear he would hug him the next moment. Fortunately, he stopped and explained:

„Every traveler is a welcome guest with us. If you are thirsty, dear human, then we have water to refresh yourself. If you feel hungry, then we will be happy to share our bread with you."

„I appreciate your offer Sir, but I really just wanted to pass by your camp and then head towards town."

The man kept his arms spread out.

„In our circle we renounce the formalities of the world out there. We are all human. No more and no less. That's why we all address each other like human that are bound in deep friendship. So, everyone is aware that he is only human among humans. No matter what he means or does outside."

He pointed towards the city.

„All this is nothing for those that gathered at this small clearing. Here we are all equal."

Now he approached MM and showed him the way to the camp by gently smiling him with one arm in the direction. Though, he did not touch him, of course MM understood the hint and voluntarily set off.

When the two entered the camp a short time later, the music fell silent, almost as a signal, and all eyes turned to MM.

„The other human in this peaceful place have just gained the freedom of their head by listening to loud meditative music. They are free of all constraints and told everything that wanted to walk the road of freedom. But now this phase is complete. Please do not be irritated. The music did not stop because of you, but because it had just reached its end."

In fact, new, but much quieter music was heard.

The man raised his voice.

„Dear human. Over there at the edge of the forest - I was just about to start looking for the fruits of the forest - my feet miraculously guided me so that I found this human by my side."

An approving murmur rose and everyone looked briefly at MM and then back to the white-bearded man.

„We want to accommodate him for a time in our circle, give him to drink, because he thirsts and give him a loaf of bread because he is hungry."

MM wanted to have corrected the strange formulation. 'We give him something to eat and drink' would have been appropriate. But he preferred to say nothing. At the same time, MM was led further into the middle of the square. The rest of the group could silently close in a circle around him.

„Please take a seat, dear human."

After MM had followed the instruction, everyone around him sat quietly on the ground and looked expectantly at the man with the flowing white hair.

‚So much for: we are all equal.' MM stated. He had run into the arms of the undisputed top guru of the group. A young man squeezed through the circle of waiting people with a small bowl of water and a small loaf of bread and laid both down in front of MM.

MMs counterpart gestured for him to eat and drink.

„I do not feel hungry or thirsty. Though I appreciate your offer, Mister."

The man's expression changed to a disappointed gaze, and it seemed to MM that everyone around him was holding his breath. After a short break, he corrected himself. „Though I appreciate your offer, my friend."

As an immediate rewarded the man smiled and a complimenting murmur came from his surroundings.

Unperturbed, the man again pointed to the food. After some reflection, MM finally took the bread in his hand and broke a piece of it. He probably would not be able to leave the camp without having eaten and drunk. So, he tried to get it over and done with, as fast as possible. After washing down the first bite with some water, he again felt the expectant eyes of everyone on him. So, he nodded approvingly.

„Well. The bread is good."

„That pleases me my dear human. If you like, you can take the rest during your stay in our relaxation camp."

MM was waiting for some more words, but nothing came. Instead, all eyes rested on him. After some hesitation, he broke another piece of bread and also ate it under a murmur of approval. MM had no idea what kind of weird club he was in here. Not wanting to lengthen the whole procedure, he also ate the rest of the bread and swallowed it with the water.

„Thank you and all of you. The water and the bread were really good."

As if all had been waiting for it, they rose and spread in the camp. Only the white-bearded man remained in front of him, still smiling. He did not give the impression of wanting to say anything in the near future. So, MM tried his luck to start a conversation. He thought it would be a good idea to do so, before he would leave the camp.

„What kind of people are you? Any peaceful sect or something?"

With tolerant expression, the man explained to him:

„If you like, we are a small group of a very big sect spanning the globe. You know the name of the sect, because you too are part of it."

After a short break for effect, he continued.

„We belong to the human."

He said these words with a significance that once again needed a little break. MM didn't know what to think.

„Actually, I already knew that you are human. Only the people - human - I knew so far behave quite differently than you do. So, what is so special about you? You have to have rules of your own that you are following."

The man thought for a while. MM was sure that it was only a question of politeness. The man wanted to give MMs question the appropriate meaning.

„We keep silence, when eating. We enjoy it when someone else can satisfy his hunger. Even if we are hungry ourselves."

Astonished, MM answered „But you do not want to tell me now that I have eaten your last bread, do you?"

„No, not at all" he smiled. „We still have plenty. Nevertheless, we are pleased to provide human with bread and water."

„That would have been an uncomfortable situation."

The man put his hand on MMs hand

„Be calm, dear human. Relax."

While MM was still thinking about how to say goodbye, without being followed by the whole group and thus attracting the attention of whomever, one of the others came and whispered something in the white-bearded man's ear, whereupon he turned back to MM.

„I have just learned that the bath is provided for you. It is our duty to offer every traveler the joy of a life-giving bath in the refreshing soils of our earth."

When MM wanted to open his mouth to refuse, the man did not let him speak. While he rose, he took MM by the arm.

„No, no, that would really be a sacrifice to our hospitality. A short time ago I have received very nervous vibrations from the group. And there it was only the modest bread and the water of the creek that you wanted to refuse. If you now say goodbye without enjoying the life-giving bath with the soils of our earth, then I'm very much afraid for the spiritual salvation of the group."

In fact, everyone had come together again and watched every movement of MM. How could he ever get away from here? If he had been sitting in his office now, he would certainly have had no mercy with these nuts. But here, without a proper suit with a painted face and disfigured ears, he felt unusually weak.

Finally, he stood in a large tent in front of a bathtub, which would have been well suited as a cow-drinking. To his horror, the tub was not filled with warm, steaming water, but with a kind of mud. Presumably it was some kind of stuff from one of the beauty temples, that women were wrapped in for expensive money. Afterwards, against better knowledge, they would determine that the skin has now become much smoother and also so very fresh.

„This is the earthen bath. It will bring refreshment for your body. Now hand me your clothes and get into the bath."

MM looked at the man in shock.

„You do not seriously think I'm going in there?"

Immediately some sobs came from the corners of the tent. Some 'human', as they called themselves, started to cry. That could not be true. Why only did this white-beard-idiot had to accost him at the edge of the forest? Why didn't he just ignore MM. He could have left him alone.

The face of the guru had changed as well. It had taken a serious and worried expression. Since MM had no idea what these 'human' would be capable of, if they would be completely overpowered by their absurd grief, he had no other choice than to give himself up. At least for the moment. He looked around the tent again.

„There are no women in this tent. This is the tent of male humans. Be assured" the white-bearded man announced.

Finally, MM undressed and climbed gently into the bathroom. The muddy, slightly reddish soup was surprisingly pleasantly warm.

„At the beginning, keep your head out of the soil, but cover all other body parts with the soils of our earth. Then the bath will unfold its unsuspected powers."

Now that he was sitting, he decided he could try to enjoy it. So, he carefully laid his head down on the edge of the bathtub and closed his eyes.

„Yes, that's exactly how to do it. In this earthen bath you can completely relax. You will remember it in many days."

It really was very pleasant. MM almost thought about apologizing at all those temples of beauty he had always despised.

„Keep your eyes closed. I will now moisten your head with the soil of our earth. I will do it with a wooden ladle. The soil should not come into your eyes."

At the same time, MM heard how the ladle was dipped. Shortly thereafter, he felt the mud flow over his stubbly bald head.

MM did not know how long it took, but eventually he was asked to get out of the tub.

„Dear human. Please position yourself there in the corner. We will rinse off the remnants of the soil with a few buckets of clear water from you."

In fact, the mud stuck to his whole body. So, he went to the corner to get cleaned up, which was not pleasant at all, since cold water was used.

„Couldn't you use warm water? Or at least warn me in advance?"

Smiling, the man explained to him: „It is part of the rite. Anyone taking this bath will be rinsed off afterwards with cold water from the creek. That closes the pores. I've forgotten to warn you. I hope you are ready to forgive me dear human."

MM, to his own amazement, did not want to argument.

„If you could hand me a towel, I would be grateful."

Only now, when MM was about to towel himself, he noticed that his entire skin had become brownish-red. Instinctively, he began to rub, without even the slightest success. He glared angrily at the still mildly smiling man.

„Do not say that I've been in Henna for just half an eternity!"

„But my dear human. That's what you did. All of us who are gathered here." As he said that, he pointed to the group of 'human' which had meanwhile gathered again. „We all were allowed to enjoy this rite. Now you too my friend. But do not worry. When this camp has reached its end in many weeks, then your skin will be back to its original color."

MM was speechless, which the man misinterpreted, however.

„Yes, you were able to experience a very important ritual of our human community in your own body: The connection with the soils of our earth."

From the group came a many-voiced „Yes, yes."

MM found it difficult to give an at least reasonably calm answer.

„You're completely crazy. The stuff will take two weeks to fade. Can you tell me what you thought?"

„Calm down my dear human. Just remember the bath. Have you ever enjoyed such a pleasant bath before?"

He looked inquiringly at MM and also the gathered other 'human' looked expectantly in his direction.

„It does not give a damn if that was relaxing or not!"

MM was back to old loudness.

„For me it is only clear that I can't be among people like that."

„But" the man replied in a mild voice „you are already wearing slightly fading symbols on your face that are done with the coils of our earth. So, you already have experience with the use of the earth. How can a bath in it have such a negative effect on your inner balance?"

„That was…" MM was able to stop himself at the last moment from explaining how it had come to his face painting. With friendly expectation, his counterpart waited for the end of the sentence begun.

„…something different" MM finished the statement, knowing that it sounded like a lame excuse. The man looked at him with a smile and then nodded after a while.

„Well, then enough is said to this matter. The day is slowly getting to its end. I suggest you get dressed again and we will retire to sleep. Because, when the sun goes to sleep, it is time for people to go to sleep as well. What is the point of being outside without the rays of sunshine?"

He led him to another tent and allocated one of the mats in the middle of the tent to him. MM pointed to a place near the exit.

„A mat on the edge would be enough for me."

„No, no. That's out of the question. Of course, you will sleep in the center. There you will be surrounded by a sense of community security."

His hands made extravagant movements that were supposed to visualize his words.

„This is like a human cocoon. Complete security. Deep, restful sleep."

MM had heard enough. He turned to the exit and tried to get out of the camp as fast as possible. To his astonishment nobody stood in his way. As if he could have done that hours ago, he ran back into the forest unmolested. He could feel the gaze of the 'human' on the back of his neck, but he did not want to turn around because he was afraid that the top guru would have taken this as an invitation to catch him again.

As he wanted to enter the woods as deep as possible, he noticed how he was scratched all over by the fir branches. When he looked down, he saw that he was still naked. How could the guy have managed to upset him so much that he needed fir branches to find he was naked? He settled himself on the thick soft layer of pine needles. What else could he do? Walking around without any clothes was definitely no option. Then he could have gone straight back to the hut to face the police. That would even have had the advantage that he would then have pretty soon got something to wear.

So, he only had the way back to the camp to the crazy humans. There he would make sure that he would get his things back and then leave the camp straight away - and this time finally. No discussion. Just dress and away.

„Welcome back my dear human. Did you want to intensify the earthen feeling on your body?"

When MM didn't answer, the white-bearded man started smiling.

„Many of us have done so. It's like an addiction that you can't put into words at the beginning. But you shouldn't walk naked outside the camp. The other human don't know to handle it."

„Actually, I just wanted to put on my things. To be honest, I don't like running around naked."

MM realized that these words did not necessarily correspond to the ideal image of intransigence. He did not understand why he appeared as such a softie. Some minutes ago, he wanted to be tough and now he was such a lame guy. The guru did not care about his problems.

„Yes, I can understand that too. After a new human of our group took the earthen bath, we all stripped ourselves in the past. But times are changing and so we don't do it anymore."

He handed MM a white fabric package.

„Take this tunic. It will cover your nakedness. We washed the clothes you wore, when you joined us. They are now clean as it should be, but unfortunately very wet."

„Why… why did you…" The very sympathetic eyes, into which MM looked as he wanted to complain, led him to the edge of his self-control. He would have preferred to have roared into the whole stupid camp and demolished the tents of these very dear 'human'. At the same time, however, he knew that he was not in his company, where he was able to enforce almost everything with the means of dismissal. Here he was surrounded by people who would probably reward every loud word as the dawn of self-liberation, with applause.

MM let his shoulders hang in resignation. He did not know at all, what was happening. In one moment he wanted to be verbally aggressive and couldn't do so. In the next moment he could scream and shout and did not.

Finally, he said:

„So, you washed my laundry. But that really wasn't necessary."

The guru raised his index finger and contradicted.

„No, no, no, my dear human. There was dirt on your clothes."

128

He made a gesture asking him to look at the other people in the camp. After a break, he added:

„And? Do you see dirt on the clothes of us human here?"

MM had to agree, whereupon the guru happily spread his arms.

„You see. And so, you too will be allowed to wear clean clothes and slip into your own clothes tomorrow morning. Or the day after tomorrow. Just as you please."

MM took a closer look at the package. The 'tunic', as the guru called it, was laced with a belt of the same material. He opened the belt and now had a sort of nightgown in his hand that he could comfortably slip over his head. To his horror, the part only went to the middle of his thighs. He had expected that it would be just over the knee, as some of the other men in the camp wore.

The guru followed his gaze and explained with a smile

„Unfortunately, this tunic is the only one we can offer. To my great shame, I must confess that we have neglected the washing service a bit over the meditation. You don't mind, do you?"

As MM pulled the belt taut, the hem slipped a little further up.

The guru took a step back and looked at MM with the gaze of a fashion designer who reflects upon the overall look of his collection for the first time on the living model.

„Well, it could have been worse. But that does not matter, because the only thing that matters is the cleanliness."

Again, he pointed to the sleeping-tent

„Now it is finally time. Once again, I have the great pleasure of inviting you to sleep together with us in our tent."

Behind the guru, MM saw two policemen approach the camp. So, without further hesitation, he accepted the offer and went to the tent. Just as he entered, he heard quick footsteps approaching. The guru stopped in front of the tent and talked with the messenger. In contradiction to the calm and confident behavior he had been showing all day, he now spoke quickly and nervously.

Finally, he turned away and moved towards the police. In the distance, MM finally heard his voice.

„I welcome you dear human. You are lucky that you still reach me. I just wanted to retire. When the sun is going to sleep, we should do so as well."

To MM it was clear that the police were looking for no one else than him. Maybe the top guru or better top jerk would be able to stop them for a while with his terrible babble, but sooner or later he would, of course, willingly lead them to that great new 'human' he had met today.

MM looked around the tent, which to his surprise was nearly empty. Nothing to see except the mats on the floor. His decision fell quickly. He could not get out in the front. There he would get into the view of the police. So, he squeezed himself under the tarpaulin on the other side. He looked around in all directions but could not see a movement anywhere. Probably all had again run to the two new human whose feet had led them so miraculously in the camp. MM could well imagine what the two policemen had to listen to at the moment. It could only be useful to him, because it gave him a small lead.

He only had to pass a few smaller tents and then had reached the edge of the forest with just a few steps. Without turning around, he went deeper into the forest. Sometime later, when he could no longer see anything because of the now complete darkness, he sat down at a tree and tried to arrange his thoughts. He was certainly wanted by the police. He had left enough genetically viable samples in the hut. He had also touched the knife that stuck in Karlssons chest. It was only a matter of time until they had a matching with his hair or whatever they could take in his house.

The logical conclusion was that he could not walk at home, in the company, or anywhere in the city. At this point his thoughts ended. Already as he fled earlier in the day through the forest and later in the camp, he had realized that. Only the top guru had managed to distract him from that topic.

How to go on? Before this stupid guru had collected him, he had at least halfway decent clothes, his IDs, and some cash.

Now he was sitting somewhere in a forest in a slightly better hospital shirt and had nothing at all. He was also covered with henna from head to toe. He would not only be extremely conspicuous because of this 'tunic'. He looked like a complete jerk or a dangerous madman. One of both. And definitely nothing in between.

In the long run, he would have no chance to hide. He did not even have the chance to get away fast. Who would take him as a hitchhiker? No chance.

But then he got an idea. Sure, he could do it. Satisfied, he lay down and tried to find sleep.

Wednesday 18th May

After breakfast, Yvonne quickly checked to see if any other emails had arrived besides spams. She was almost hoping that the blackmailer would get in touch again. But there was nothing in the mailbox. So, as in the last few days, she turned back to cleaning the house. The hot clothes and high heels had almost become her habit. Still, she was not enjoying life at the moment. She has gotten rid of MM and his humiliations. Yes, that was good. At least for some days. Somehow, she was sure, that the blackmailer would do him no serious harm. Everything was fine so far. But now there was a certain emptiness, which had to be filled. Insofar, she was glad that she at least had the job at Beatrice' shop. Maybe Beatrice could even become a real friend.

When she finally could not stand it in the house, she considered to drive into the city to do a little window shopping and maybe then to take a coffee with Beatrice. At that moment the phone rang.

***

MM tried to find the way back to the camp. This time he looked around carefully. In no case did he want to bump into the guru again. Who knows what he would do to him this time and what he had said yesterday to the police. Since he did not know the way he had walked during the night, he had to try his luck. The only thing he was sure of was that he had not crossed wide trails at night. As a result, after some time, he managed to limit the area in which the clearing with the camp had to be located.

When he finally spotted it among the trees, he almost let out a cheer. Now he had to walk on a large-scale bow around the camp. He counted his steps and stopped after every tenth to watch out carefully. This strategy would make him stay longer in the danger zone, but on the other hand, it also reduced the risk of overlooking any person from the camp who might be in the woods to catch any new inspiration.

After half an eternity, he finally had his goal. The 'human' had, as he had already seen yesterday, arrived with something as banal as cars. There they stood united in front of him. All inferior quality, but he had expected nothing else. Even a 2CV was there. That actually belonged to the museum. Now the riskiest part of his plan started, and at the same time, the part where the plan could fail completely because stealing cars was none of his business. He started checking all the cars. As he had expected, almost no car was locked. Unfortunately, nobody had left the key.

Having once heard of a story where a car key was simply placed on one of the tires, he also checked that on each of the cars. When he was almost through, he held the key of the 2CV in his hand. He did not think long. Plugging in and starting was almost a single move. Now he had to drive away with as little engine noise as possible. Although he had little hope that he was not to be heard. But perhaps they were just floating in the seventh heaven of meditation and did not care about the typical sound of a departing 2CV. He could only hope. To his delight, the fuel gauge showed him that the tank was almost completely filled. Though he did not know what that meant in kilometers, it was a good signal. Without real orientation, he drove out of the forest and then tried to slowly but surely move away from the city with frequent changes of roads. After an hour he reached a forest again, where he stopped in a lonely parking lot and took the time to search the interior space. Maybe there were a few euros or even reasonable clothes in the car.

The glove box was empty except for a few papers. Finally, he found a filled backpack in the trunk. He could barely believe his luck as he pulled out of the side pocket a cell phone that was switched on. He was able to call Yvonne and order her with a set of new suits. Only that had to wait until he found a spot that Yvonne was able to find. The backpack contained pieces of clothing that, to his great disappointment, were clearly not made for men. Not that he thought that silly tunic was a garment for men, but skirts and blouses were certainly even more inappropriate.

***

He stopped in one of the parking garages in the next big city and dialed Yvonne's number.

„MM speaking. Take a note and write down what I need."

Without waiting for her answer, he gave her an extensive list.

„That's all?" Yvonne wanted to know, when he stopped speaking.

„I do not know what else I could need. Don't potter. Get that together as quick as possible. Shouldn't be to hard. Then you are allowed to take my car and join me here in my parking garage. I expect you in two hours."

With that he ended the call.

With a smile on her face, Yvonne wondered if MM thought 'my parking garage' was a place the navigation system of his car would be able to find. She started to fetch the suitcases and fill them with clothes and suits. When she had finished, the phone rang again and MM gave her the information where to find him.

She arrived with an hour late at MM, who drew attention with flashers. Because of his outfit, he had to stay in the car. He opened the side window

„Is that really that hard to arrive on schedule? Didn't you realize the situation I'm in? It's really complicated. One more reason for you, to do your very best."

Yvonne had expected that he would at least thank her.

„Hello MM. Nice to see you again."

She leaned forward to get a better look at him.

„Another layer henna?"

Automatically he tried to move back into the shadow.

„Ok, ok, it's ok. Did you at least get everything?"

„Of course. I suggest that you abandon that wonderful 2CV to its fate and join me."

„How do you get the idea that we go back together? I'm too busy to struggle with you and your ideas."

When MM got out of the 2CV, Yvonne took a step back and whistled approvingly.

„Hot outfit. You know how to dress up."

„If you do not want to be slapped, then just shut up."

His look fell on Yvonne's collar.

„What's that? Are you completely nuts or something? Is that any stupid solidarity thing? Just because I was treated badly, you do not have to do such a crap."

Yvonne laid her hand at her collar and smilingly told him that this was the latest fashion trend.

„I have no time for such silly bullshit now. You put everything in the trunk?"

„Yes, Sir. Everything as ordered, Sir" Yvonne answered in military intonation.

She pulled a cell phone out of her pocket.

„And here is a prepaid phone. Everything unlocked. The code is 4711."

MM took the phone

„The car keys?"

„Ignition lock. What about the 2CV? Should I drive with it now?"

„If you have enough cash for the parking ticket. Have fun."

He climbed into his beloved luxury car and accelerated.

***

„ You really do not have an easy time with MM. Well, someday I'll catch him and have a serious word with him. Too bad he did not want to fly to Edinburgh. I had thought of some nice things for him. Well, I'll stay in touch with you."

As Yvonne read the mail the doorbell rang.

When she opened, the two police officers were at the door again.

„Good evening Mrs. Müller. Is her husband at home?"

„No."

„You can't possibly tell us where we can find him or how we can reach him?"

„My husband called me at lunchtime and asked me to bring him some things. I just came back. Unfortunately, I can't tell you where he is now. But he told me that you are looking for him. And he also told me that I am not obliged to help you. After that, he drove away with his car and I could go back with a 2CV, which he picked up from some friends or elsewhere. Was no time to ask him."

„When did you meet your husband?"

„This afternoon at 3:55."

„Would you give us a call when your husband gets in touch with you the next time?"

„Although I really can't speak well of him right now, if I agree, I would do something that I'm not really committed to as his wife. Or am I wrong?"

Smidt already nodded.

„No, no, you don't have to do so. However, we will certainly come back several times if there are any further questions you can answer."

Smidt turned to go and had to nudge her colleague, as he could not take his eyes off Yvonne's collar.

„Oh, the car you just talked about. I would like to see that."

Yvonne pointed to the other side of the street

„The 2CV. You can't miss it."

While the two of them went to the car, DS Rednich pulled out his cell phone.

„DS Rednich, I have an inquiry."

Since Yvonne did not want to appear curious, she closed the door. Just a few minutes later the two officers rang the bell again.

„The car seems to be stolen. Now you would have to give more details. We can come in?"

The frustration was quick to notice. Yvonne couldn't do more than to tell them about the parking garage. She reassured them that she had never expected MM to become a thief.

„Even if it does not look like. Maybe there is a harmless explanation?"

Yvonne did not believe it herself. So much had gone wrong in the last few days. Why shouldn't he become a thief, too?

When the two of them put up a regretful expression instead of answering, Yvonne questioned what would happen to the 2CV.

„The owner will pick it up himself. He doesn't want to report because he assumes that your husband must have acted in a real emergency."

They gave no answer to Yvonne's incredulous amazement. They just got up and left the house.

***

„Hello, who is it?" MM had not even registered that his cell phone was ringing. Since no one except Yvonne could have his number, and he did not expect a phone call from Yvonne, he had completely forgotten that he had a phone.

„It's me. The person who has been causing you so much stress in the last few days."

With that, MMs mental fatigue disappeared abruptly.

„Then tell me who you are and what I should do, so that all this finally stops. You even blamed me for the murder of Triebel and I'm sure you'll also try to blame me for Karlsson death. So, this is the moment to put your cards on the table. How do we get into business?"

There was a pause until the voice answered.

„You're a little too fast with your questions. At least I would like to introduce myself. I am a synthetically created voice. So, you do not have to think about hearing the distorted voice of anyone you know. Since each of my words must be generated by a written text, we should quickly get to the heart of the conversation. Otherwise it will drag on, because from now on no ready-made answers will be available anymore."

MM had indeed hoped that if they spoke only long enough, he would recognize the voice. He was now deprived of this hope.

„Okay? What's the deal?"

After a long break came the answer.

„A self-denunciation would be a solution. I'd leave you alone instantly."

This was to stupid to be answered. MM was sure that the blackmailer knew it.

„Where did you get my number from? Did Yvonne blab?"

Again, the answer came after a break.

„Yvonne did not blabber, but I can modestly say that I am talented in these matters."

„Is it about money? Do you want money? Tell me the amount and you will get it, if you assure beforehand that you make it clear to the police that I have nothing to do with Triebels death."

MM counted to 30. Then finally the answer came.

„You still do not understand the basic problem. Money does not matter to me. However, what you have understood is that I am able to get you out of the police investigation. Congratulations! You were able to understand at least a little bit. Not everyone likes to sit in prison for murder. Especially if he did not commit it."

MM had to struggle with himself until he asked the question that the blackmailer apparently wanted to hear.

„If it is not the money, what can I do to clear my name from murder suspicion? There must be a solution. Say it and I will do it if it is in my power."

This time he had to wait a minute for the answer.

„Well, there is indeed an alternative …"

***

„Hi Beatrice. How are you?"

Of course, Yvonne knew that she was far too late for her cleaning service.

„You're late sweet Yvonne. I hope, you have a real good story for me."

Yvonne rolled her eyes.

„Just stop it. To make a long story short: MM ordered me to Stuttgart, to bring him a bunch of his clothes. I completely forgot to inform you."

„Would have been better. Though we are friends, we also have a contract that we both must comply. A short call would have been enough."

„How can I make amends? Cleaning with chains again or something?"

„We might think about professional cleaning later. Now it's just time that you work off your guilt."

Beatrice went back and gestured for Yvonne to come along. She took a black tube with corset-like lacing from a box. Only this part was cut much tighter than a corset.

„Already seen?"

Yvonne shook her head.

„This is a mono glove. Today you will wear it during your cleaning hours. After that, it's settled. OK?"

Yvonne was not sure.

„In principle, okay, but how do I wear it? I don't really have an idea."

„Just turn around and put your hands behind your back."

No sooner Beatrice was pulling the glove up Yvonne's arms. Since the lacing was completely open, that was very easy and not unpleasant.

„So now I put the two straps over your shoulders and put them back on the glove. If I wouldn't do that, the glove might slip down and of course that is strictly forbidden."

While Beatrice explained it, she already fixed the straps. As Yvonne looked at her shoulders, she felt reminded of backpack straps. So, if the glove was annoying, she would still be able to strip off the straps and then somehow make sure the glove slid down her arm. Although Beatrice had said otherwise. At the same time, she realized that it would not come to that, since she trusted Beatrice.

While Yvonne was lost in thoughts about her escape-possibilities, Beatrice had already completed the first round of tightening. Like a corset, the two edges of the glove slowly moved toward each other, forcing the elbows closer together. Since Yvonne had always been flexible, that was not a real problem for a while. It was not until Beatrice announced that it now needed only one more passage until the glove was completely closed, she objected.

„I do not think I can stand this for hours if you make it even tighter."

„I was surprised that you did not complain earlier. It's pretty tight for the first time. Listen to exactly what I say: If you notice that your hands or arms are no longer properly supplied with blood, then contact me. I'll take the glove off immediately. I don't want you to get any damage from it."

„All right. What should I do now? Cleaning is no option. Obviously."

„Actually, an easy job. I'll show you."

She led Yvonne back to the store and let her get into a tall cage that usually hung from the ceiling, but this time it was lowered to the floor.

Beatrice smiled and made a welcoming gesture.

„Get in and enjoy."

As soon as Yvonne was in the cage, Beatrice had already locked the door and activated the winch by remote control, until the cage was about 3 meters high.

„Just stay in the cage until I get you down again and enjoy the looks of the customers. If you get bored, you can count the mono-gloves I sell during that time."

Yvonne was too surprised to give her an answer. In addition, some customers had just entered the shop and inspected her.

„No cleaning today?"

Yvonne had not imagined that at all. She just came to the store to chat a bit with Beatrice and do her cleaning-job maybe with some special garments. And now, at least for a few hours, she found herself helplessly trapped in a cage and was also approached by the customers. She looked to Beatrice for help, but Beatrice only smiled happily and told her that she is asked to talk to the customer who had spoken to her. Why not? After all, time goes by faster when you have something to do, even if it's just small talk.

Thursday 19th May

Yvonne had just sat down to have a cozy breakfast when MM called.

„I absolutely have to meet you today. Exactly 1 p.m. at the forest parking lot. You know. The one we always take."

„Should I bring you something again? Maybe some suits?

After a short hesitation, he listed a few articles and then interrupted the line. Last words were that he wanted to prevent being located.

Before Yvonne took the first sip of coffee, she informed Beatrice that she would be late again. Though hanging around in the cage has definitely been a very special experience, she did not want to risk a new penalty.

She decided to leave early enough to make the purchases and then drive directly to the indicated meeting point. In the supermarket however, she had to remember what he wanted, as she had left the note in the kitchen. When she finally got everything, she started running out of time. Her purchases were already on the conveyor belt when the customer in front of her calmly took out her purse and began to count the desired amount in small coins. The cashier watched her actions with great patience.

„Now 15 cents are still needed."

The customer looked again in her purse and shook her head with regret.

„No chance. Such an annoyance. I didn't want to pay with a fresh banknote today. Once you start them, they're gone. Better use coins as long as possible."

She thoughtfully rubbed her chin.

„Oh, I always have a few coins in my coat pocket."

She looked at the cashier without knowing if she understood the reason.

„You know, all the beggars who appeal to you on the street. You shouldn't show the whole purse. After all, these can be crooks who are only looking for it."

To Yvonne's relief, the woman fetched a few cents out of her pocket and put them to the other coins. When the cashier wanted to take it, she was stopped by the woman

„Just a moment young lady. I have added 20 cents. So, I have to get 5 cent back"

„I would have noticed that" the cashier assured.

„Well, if you notice it yourself, you can do it directly."

She took the coin with a happy smile

„All done."

Yvonne wouldn't have been surprised if she had held up the 5-cent coin triumphantly.

When Yvonne finally got to the car, she had hardly enough time to get to the forest parking lot on time. So, when she had finally left the city, she stepped on the gas. Unfortunately, she hadn't thought about the speed camera. MM would probably freak again. On the other hand. He had to face problems that were far beyond a speed ticket. In addition, she was thinking more and more about a divorce anyway. When she thought about it, she didn't really know why she was driving to the forest parking lot. Again, MM wouldn't say 'thank you' and instead accuse her of something she had done wrong again. On the other hand, she was almost already there. So, she could finish it.

She arrived in the parking lot just a minute late. Besides her, there was only one other car, a small van. Probably some workers enjoyed an extended lunch break. There was nothing to see from MM. She decided to take a little lap across the parking lot. Maybe he was hiding somewhere. After all, his whole head was painted with henna.

She had no idea where the hand with the rag came from. When she tried to fight back, she realized that her strength was slackening.

***

„I think with the cage and the monoglove I exaggerated it yesterday. Yvonne just told me this morning, that she would come later, because she would have to do something important for her stupid MM again and then she did not come at all."

As usual, Rondo had welcomed her with the prepared dinner. He looked at her thoughtfully

„And why do you think it was your treatment? Maybe MM was thinking only of himself and now she is stuck somewhere. Wouldn't be the first time."

„Yes, but then at least she would answer the cell phone. But it's only the mailbox. Believe me, she's probably pissed because of yesterday."

„It only took a few days to fire her up about all the stuff you're selling, and she didn't object when you put her in chains for cleaning. And all that happened, as I said, in no time. The employment contract can be easily torn to pieces by any law student. And this will be clear for her. I do not think such a person will just get out, all of a sudden. And even if she would do it, she would get in touch beforehand. I think she will show up tomorrow in your shop and explain, that MM once again did a few unplanned selfish things."

Beatrice smiled.

„Then I can already think about the punishment that she will receive tomorrow. Maybe next time she will be able to say NO to MM."

„Ok. Let's just finish eating and then it's off to the game room."

Friday 20ᵗʰ May

The grey fog lifted very slowly. Her eyes didn't really want to obey her yet. Since she was lying on her back, it was perfectly logical for Yvonne that the eyes had to follow gravity and therefore could only be held in the middle with extreme concentration. She had in mind her old physics teacher, who was just explaining the 'labile balance'. All she had to do was to make sure that the eyes gravity center went down. The solution was very simple. She just had to turn on her stomach. Then the eyes would be at the bottom and automatically pulled in a straight direction by gravity. Trying to turn around, she fell back to sleep.

The next time she woke up, the thoughts concerning the balance of her eyes were forgotten. She still felt tired, but the fog in front of her head and in her head had nearly cleared. Only a hardly visible veil of mist was left. So far so good. But now she realized that something was completely wrong. She was lying in a room she didn't know. What had happened? What had she done before she fell asleep? The last thing she remembered was that MM had called her to a stupid meeting. She couldn't find more in her memory.

She looked around. The room was spacious, clean and tastefully decorated. The window opened up the view of a green pasture landscape with some adjacent wooded areas. Someone had dressed her in a long nightgown that reached down to her feet and even further. She had to lift the lower part so as not to accidentally stumble over it. Her eyes fell on her fingernails. The familiar silver-glossy nails had disappeared and were replaced by slightly longer nails, which had a dark red stripe in the middle and were painted white on the outside. Even more surprising, however, were the painting of her hands. The back of her hand and fingers were covered by an ornate henna tattoo.

She automatically grabbed her nose and ears to see if she now was wearing lots of piercings. To her relief, however, she found that at least her head has been left alone. So, she continued to explore the room. When she opened the large wardrobe, she felt like she was looking into the wardrobe of an old swashbuckler movie. There was not a single normal garment to be seen. Instead, underwear and long skirts from long past centuries. Even corsets were to be found.

If someone had told her that she would be kidnapped one day, she would have expected to wake up somewhere in a hole or a damp cellar. Somebody would be there to explain the hopelessness of her situation and begin to treat her in some nasty, rude and painful way. She would have never expected that this special blackmailer would ever come up with the idea to kidnap her.

But now it obviously had happened and she found herself in a complete unexpected situation. A clean room, furnished with impeccable furniture. More like an apartment than a prison. There were two doors in her room. What did she have to lose? There was certainly someone watching her with a hidden camera anyway. If he wanted her something to do or not to do, he would come forward with his proposals. She carefully pushed down the handle of the first door. Locked. The second door, however, could be opened. It led to a small kitchen and from there to a small living room, which was equipped with a large bookcase and even a TV. Only the windows were missing. Instead, there were bright fabrics with some indirect lightning. When she gently pushed the fabric to the side, she noticed that the window was bricked up. After all, they had made an effort. Better than a bare bricked-up window surface.

Behind another door, she found the bathroom, which was also fully equipped to her relief. Even all the cosmetics she used were completely present. Automatically, she nodding her head. Luckily, he hadn't come up with the idea of getting the equipment from the time, the clothes in the closet belonged.

For the moment she had seen enough. Yvonne returned to the first room. She could not remember ever hearing of a kidnapping in which the victim had been kept in such an apartment. She knew it wasn't right, but somehow, she felt good. According to her hunger, she had probably eaten nothing for a long time. Since no one seemed to care for her, she decided to check the kitchen. To her astonishment, she found not only cupboards containing rice, pasta and plenty of canned vegetables. In the fridge even a fresh salad was waiting for her. Really hard to believe, but that was reality. She took time to prepare a meal. Now she realized what it means to work with nails that were again half a centimeter longer. Getting used to it would take some time. Her kidnapper seemed to have a fetish with that.

After eating and rinsing, she sat down in the living room, indiscriminately took a book off the shelf and began reading.

Saturday 21st May

When she woke up the next morning, her situation had not changed. She continued to intend to act as if everything was normal. So, she went to the bathroom to take a shower. As she had to admit, this was more than necessary. When she could barely keep her eyes open in the evening before, she had only crawled into bed and had fallen into a deep sleep.

In the bathroom, she stripped naked and noticed to her astonishment that she was completely hairless. The only explanation she had for not recognizing it yesterday was the anesthetic. Obviously, she hasn't been as clear in her brain as she had thought. She turned back and forth in front of the mirror, but apart from the hair on her head, she couldn't find a single hair. Well, then. Let's see what other surprises the kidnapper had in store for her. The henna painting, as she now noted, went slightly up to half of the forearms. She didn't notice that yesterday either. All right. Now she felt completely fit and was sure to have examined her entire body for changes. So, there couldn't be any more surprises waiting for her.

After the shower, she realized that she hadn't taken any clothes into the bathroom. Since she had dropped the nightgown already into the laundry basket, she walked naked to the wardrobe. Hoping that she might have missed something here yesterday, e.g. a shelf with practical normal clothes, she opened the doors. However, she found that she had not overlooked anything. Underwear that was so generously cut that you could certainly have cut a dozen modern briefs out of one single pair of underpants - she didn't want to think of thongs. And lots of dresses that ended up in long skirts. Apart from the corsets, nothing else was to be found.

All she could do was walk around naked all day, put on the sweaty nightgown or try one of the clothes. Why not? No one seemed to contact her again, so she had to face a long day that wanted to be filled with activities. Randomly she took a dress and one of the bombastic underpants. Her underpants went almost to her knees and were so out of fashion that they were nearly good again. Hoping that she would think the same about the dress, she took it off the handle. Her gaze fell on a piece of paper, which was loosely attached to the collar of the dress.

„Dear Yvonne, you will find such an instruction on every one of these wonderful dresses. The dresses are cut quite waisted, so it is necessary that you wear them together with a corset. You have had some experience with these garments recently. This will now be to your advantage, as you have to tie these wonderful pieces of laundry up by yourself. You will notice that the corsets in the closure area have some additional metal closures that will automatically snap in when they are close enough to their counterpart. So, it's easy for you to decide when you've pulled the lacing tight enough. Simply when everything is locked in. If you're wondering how to reopen them. This is actually quite simple. You take a deep breath and open the front closing of the corset.

I don't think you come up with the idea of not following my instructions, but I want to warn you anyway. If you wear one of these wonderful dresses without a properly laced corset, I will have to punish you.

But now again to the pleasant things of life. The corset number 5 fits perfectly with this dress. With the shoes, I leave you free choice. But please don't go barefoot, otherwise the hem of the dress would drag all day long.

Now all that remains is for me to wish you a pleasant day."

This guy had to have a fair amount of clutter in his head. Yvonne pondered how someone could have the motivation to prepare all this for her and then just enjoy seeing her locked up here, like an animal in a small zoo. After all, he had great confidence in her behavior. There were enough knifes in the kitchen to turn the contents of the wardrobe into a perfect job for the garbage container. She could also try to break open the door or the window. Nevertheless, she felt a kind of sympathy for him. So far, he had done nothing really bad to her. She was sure that he would not do so in the future, as long as she did not give him a reason to do so.

While she was following these considerations, she had already pulled out the designated corset. She closed the corset by hooking up the front locking strip. Afterwards, she began to tighten the lace on her back. When all the locks were finally locked in, she felt the tightness she already knew, but was not overly constricted.

The dress, which was also closed with a lacing, fitted absolutely perfect. However, the hem was actually too long. When she put on shoes with 10cm heels, the problem was solved and she had to think about how she wanted to spend the rest of the day.

An inspection of the living room revealed a radio hidden in the closet, which, to her delight, had all channels. She was sure that would make the day reasonable. Let's see when the kidnapper would come forward.

***

It was not the first time that Beatrice was at Yvonne's door and rang. Again, no one was at home. A glance through the kitchen window showed that the dishwasher door was still open at the same angle as yesterday. Since she knew of Yvonne's clean-up madness by now, this was proof enough for her. Yvonne was not home and hadn't been there since her last inspection.

Just as she was about to leave, a typical police middle-class car drove into the driveway. The person who got out was the last one she had expected here. Apparently Rednich was no different.

„Beatrice? What are you doing here?"

„Günther! If I didn't already have an idea, I could ask you the same thing."

She walked towards Rednich with joy. As they hugged briefly, she began to inquire about his well-being.

„Generally speaking, I'm all right. It's always the same. Only names and locations are changing. But seeing you here surprises me."

„As a good police officer, you will probably sooner or later find out that Yvonne and I have been befriending each other a little in the last few weeks. She is a really nice person, but unfortunately she is also the cliché of the frustrated wife of a rich man who actually only needs her for household and representation."

„And you took a little care of her?"

A worry line appeared on his forehead.

„Don't make such an uprising out of it. Sexy clothes and a bit of bondage can be really fun. Of course, only if you are not forced to do so. I was just a bit unlucky back then. Maybe I was just waiting for it. I don't know." After a short break, she added with joy „Anyway, I'm doing brilliantly now."

„Well, if that's the case, then everything is fine with you. I'm happy to hear that."

„Let's stop talking about us for the moment." She looked back at the house. „I'm worried about Yvonne. In fact, she should have been in touch some time ago. I fear that she has been forced in a situation that she cannot control."

„Since when do you miss her?"

„She called me on Thursday. Told me that she would come to my shop a little later, because she would have to do something for her stupid husband beforehand. I haven't heard from her since."

„So, she had contact with her husband?"

„Apparently. At least that's what she told me. But please tell me what you are doing here."

Rednich automatically began to step uncomfortably from one foot to the other.

„You know. The police are always allowed to ask everyone and everyone should answer well, but the other way around, the game only works if the police wants to play tricks on you."

„I suppose you're looking for Yvonne's husband?"

Immediately, he stopped his movements and waited anxiously for her next step.

„Listen. I'm really worried about Yvonne. I know, of course, that I'm not close enough to her to trigger a police operation, but I'm sure that I'm right. If you are looking for her husband, you should finally enter this house here. Nobody lives here at the moment. If I'm not completely wrong, you'll find a computer with a lot of investigative material."

„If you know anything about the case, this is your moment."

„Yvonne has told something about blackmail. That's why she and her husband have been visiting a few cities recently. I don't know any specific things."

The two looked at each other in silence for a while until Rednich rose to speak again.

„I really regretted that you left at the time. A solution could have been found."

Beatrice smiled.

„Let the old things rest. As I have just told you, I am happy with the life I lead now. And that's worth a lot, isn't it?"

Rednich hugged her again.

„You're right. That is the main thing. I would like to hope that your concern for Mrs. Müller will prove to be without any reason. How can I reach you if I need your help?"

„I have a shop. I'm in the internet. As a good cop, this clue must be enough for you", she answered him with a small laugh. But then she handed him her business card. „And you? How do I reach you?"

Rednich smiled and gave her his card in exchange.

„You would have been able to find the number. After all, you once belonged to us."

Sunday 22nd May

„I'm waiting for your call all the time. I have done everything you asked for. What about your promise now? Can I go out in public? Yes or no! My shops have been without my supervision long enough!"

Again, MM couldn't bear that this unfortunate pause arose until the computer voice answered him.

„Dear MM. You are too impatient. I did everything I could. One more night and you can return to your beloved house. That's something, isn't it?"

„Why another night? Do you have any idea how I'm doing here? No fresh clothes! No clean table! I have to do everything on my own!"

Instead of pause with the following answer, he only heard that the call had been ended. If anything was certain for MM, it was that he would get this nasty little blackmailer in his fingers and then ruin him in such a way that he wouldn't take root for the rest of his miserable life.

He looked around in the hut, which he had found by chance. Nothing but a bed that didn't really deserve the name, a table and a chair. At least there was a creek with some clear water and some shrubs with berries nearby. As long as he could drink, nothing bad would happen for several days. Nevertheless, he was extremely annoyed that he was forced to rejoice because he had found such a run-down hut. Just a few kilometers away, a house with all the luxury was waiting for him. Nevertheless, he had to stay in this shelter for another night. He would have enjoyed to shout out his anger. But he couldn't allow himself to do so. That made him even more angry.

***

Beatrice sat in the garden with Rondo. Since there had been no opportunity to tell him about her talk with Rednich, she had just made up for it.

Rondo looked at her thoughtfully.

„Do you think they really don't care about Yvonne?"

„I can't tell. Rednich has always been a totally fair colleague but like his name says: Not talking much. On the other hand, he was always known for being very mindful. I have the impression that this hasn't changed."

„And now?" Rondo looked at her inquiringly. „What are we going to do?"

„If Rednich or the team are also concerned about Yvonne's whereabouts, you can be sure that Rednich will talk about the little chat with me and that they are trying to record the track. If Yvonne or my tip is not of interest to the team, then we will know tomorrow at the latest."

„Why? You just said, that Rednich won't talk. So, he certainly won't call you to tell you what they've decided in the team."

„Yeah, but I think we're taking a short stroll with a picnic in the park opposite Yvonne's house."

Rondo nodded appreciatively. A short time later, they had packed everything they needed and set off.

What could be better than lying comfortably in the shade of a large tree on the lawn. The cooler bag was filled with drinks and a few little things to eat, Beatrice had put her head on Rondo's thigh and let herself be fondled extensively. All she had to do was make sure she didn't fall asleep and thus miss her former colleagues.

„You know 'Smoke on the water'?" Rondo wanted to know. „And fire in the sky" Beatrice continued the text.

„Of course, I know that. Isn't that a song about some idiots who have set such a lake stage in Switzerland on fire when Frank Zappa was playing?"

„Almost. It was the casino of Montreux that had burned down. But it is true that it happened at a concert of Zappa."

„And why is it called 'smoke on the water'? I always thought that meant some lake?"

„Yes, but only because the smoke was drawn over the lake."

Beatrice continued to look at Yvonne's house.

„How did 'smoke on the water' come into your mind?"

„I came across some really good concerts by Jon Lord. Like a symphonically orchestra with violins and all that stuff. Unfortunately, he is already dead. I really missed something."

Beatrice looked at Rondo.

„From rock musician to classical composer?"

Rondo smiled.

„I have some pieces of those on my player. Want to hear?"

Beatrice could never have imagined that she could forget herself in music like this.

Monday 23rd May

To his relief, the henna on his face could only be seen as a kind of skin impurity. Believing in the promise of the blackmailer, he had returned home at around 7 a.m. First thing to do was to take a shower. He had originally planned to shower until the hot-water tank was empty, but after half an hour he stopped.

He then walked through the house in a bathrobe to see if anything had changed. He was interrupted by the doorbell. Still feeling good to be clean again, he opened the door. In front of him stood two people who could only be police officers.

„It is nice to finally see you Mr. Müller. We have been looking for you for some time and I have to say that until yesterday this would have meant: custody."

The time it took Smidt to pronounce the two sentences was enough for MM to recover from the shock. He managed to turn his facial expression to a questioning expression.

„May I know who you are?"

„Oh, completely forgotten. My name is Smidt and this is my colleague DC Rednich."

Both pulled out their IDs and held them up mechanically for a brief moment, while Smidt continued to talk.

„I am astonished that you haven't already contacted us yourself. After all, you are involved in a murder investigation."

She looked around to show him that they were still in public.

„We would like to ask you a few more questions. If you don't mind inviting us in for a moment, we can now put it right behind us. Otherwise, we must ask you to visit us in the Headquarter."

She pulled a letter envelope from her briefcase and looked at him inquiringly.

„I think I prefer to visit the Headquarter. Accompanied by my lawyer, of course."

„Naturally." She handed him the envelope and held him a form on which he acknowledged its receipt. „In order to avoid wasting time, I would also like to give you a quick view at what will be the beginning of our conversation."

She briefly confronted him with one of the pictures taken in Luxembourg. The two officers then turned to the road. Not visible to MM, Smidt counted the seconds with her fingers. When she arrived at four, MM asked them in.

„What exactly do you want to know?"

They were now sitting in the same room where Yvonne had talked with them. Although Rednich didn't particularly like the clothes Yvonne had worn, she had looked much better than her husband. MM wore no clothes under the bathrobe and carelessly kept his legs so far apart that they had a comprehensive insight into his intimate region.

„You don't give an impression like you're having a lot of routine or even fun. How is it that you did it anyway?"

„I don't know why I should answer that question."

„Perhaps because the murdered Mr. Triebel had just been charged with a blackmail case. We needed a little bit, but in the end, we got the loose ends together. You seem to be the client and the blackmail victim at the same time."

MM looked at her „and?"

„At the crime scene there were some traces that steered us in your direction. However, as suspect. Yesterday we got a huge bunch of photos and videos in which you are without exception the main actor. What I have shown is just one of them. Some of the material is well suited to acquit you from the suspicion of murder to the detriment of..." Smidt broke off and looked slightly amused to Rednich. „So, to acquit you of the suspicion that you killed Triebel. Some of the material is just what it is. Namely, photos of someone walking around in public in clothes made of latex and rubber. Perhaps you have proclaimed yourself with a lot of self-conquest to your presumably long-secret love for this kind of clothing. Your first public appearance?"

She had watched MMs face all the time. She recognized the pale patterns on his skin and the fresh holes in his ears. She made sure that he could follow her gaze. This and the hint of what material she had in her hands did not miss its effect on MM. He became increasingly red and finally jumped up.

„Get out of here. How dare you! Don't stick your nose into my private affairs! If you ever have anything concrete against me, then you can come back! But not a minute earlier!"

When they rose, Smidt asked: „Where is your wife?"

MM stopped in its movement for a fraction of a second.

„What do I know? Probably again with a friend. Drift from one spot to the next. In any case, she did not tell me where she is. She will come back somewhen."

„Since when has she gone?"

MM tried to push them towards the door.

„What do I know? I wasn't there for a few days and I hadn't had any contact with her."

„Doesn't she have a mobile phone?"

„Stop asking! You're allowed to act like this?"

By now they had arrived at the door. Just as Rednich was about to open the door, his gaze fell on his shoelaces, one of which had opened. He bent down to fix it.

„Of course, I'm allowed to ask you that. But actually the question is redundant, because..." she shrugged her shoulders „who doesn't have a mobile phone these days?"

„Millions of guys in primeval forests and other strange places, for example!"

„It's nice that you've kept your sense of humor. There are some who don't put something like this away so easily."

MM stared at her in silence.

„I mean, let's take such funny pictures and then all of a sudden the wife is no longer there."

He was still just staring at her.

„Don't worry about your wife?"

„You keep asking and continuing to ask. That's your strategy? I have already told you that you're not welcome here!"

He looked at Rednich, who had finally finished his knot and opened the door.

„What actually happened to your ears? It looks terrible."

Smidt looked at MM with real concern. He automatically grabbed his ears and visibly struggled for an answer.

"An accident." When the pitying glances of the two officers made it clear to him that they refused to belief this explanation, he added "something like that"

"I would recommend that you sue the piercer. Everyone can see that you are not the type for such earrings. He should have refused. The least he would have done would have been to make an appointment for the next day. So that you could have thought one last time."

She could see how uncomfortable he was about this subject.

"May I ask you if you were drunk when you got those piercings? They are even made with a really thick hollow needle. This will certainly not grow together. If the guy would have done at least normal holes, that would be forgotten in a few days. But now…"

MM could hardly suck it up.

"Go! Dare to come back!"

He watched the two of them until they got into their car and disappeared from his sight.

He desperately needed a new private investigator. Karlsson would have never been a permanent replacement for Triebel anyway. He had always been the man for the rough stuff. Now he absolutely needed someone with brains. Determined, he took out the yellow pages and searched for detectives. Right at the first number he called, the 'no connection to this number'-tape came up. A glance at the first page showed him that the yellow pages were already 10 years old. How could it be that Yvonne was too lazy to keep the phone books up-to-date?

The answer was on the desk in the office. She had a fondness for the Internet. Surely there was also a phone book. For the first time, he was annoyed that he had always steadfastly refused to get to know at least the basic things on the Internet. Yvonne had offered it to him more than once and had finally given up.

Reluctantly, he opened the device. Fortunately, he didn't have to enter a password. He had snapped up the appearance of one of the Internet programs again and again. He boldly clicked on the icon. Fortunately, the Internet immediately responded by asking him to enter the term he was looking for. Just as he was about to type in 'Private Detective', another piece of information appeared on the screen that told him that he had received seven new emails.

After a moment, he clicked "Read". What did he expect? In addition to a few unimportant mails for Yvonne, the blackmailer was also there again.

„Dear MM. I don't even want to give the impression that I could also greet Yvonne in this way. At the moment I probably know a lot better than you where she is. If you're interested in that, I'd like to tell you that she's doing well.

However, this is not the reason for this mail. When I realized, to my great joy, that you are now actually dealing with a real computer, contrary to your previous behavior, I couldn't help but send you an e-mail.

But now I'll stop with the little jokes and teasing. Let us move on to the essential content of my message: You have already learned from the two nice officers who have just visited you that there are extensive picture and sound documents of your actions. Far more, by the way, if I may explain this to you with some pride, than the two officers have in their hands. Some of these documents are made with such foresight that they unquestionably clear you from the suspicion of killing a certain gentleman called Triebel. Did you know that he indeed tried to track me down? Outrageous.

So far so good. There are other documents that, if I deftly remove them from the context, are quite suitable to get one or the other average-thinking person to think that you might have had an interest in causing the death of Triebel. As we all know as law-abiding citizens, not only the one who carries out the act, but also the one who ordered the act has to be pleaded guilty in accordance with our laws. But I don't want to go so

160

far as to blame you for things that you are not responsible for. There is such a plentiful source of actions for which you bear the responsibility and which did not lead directly to murders, but are nevertheless punishable.

If you're wondering if I'm bluffing, I'll tell you that an excellent bureaucrat has been lost with Triebels death. One of the characteristics of the Germans, which is highly valued by many peoples of the world, is this correct work and this obsession to document everything cleanly. Not that I think everyone in this country is like that, but a lot of people around the world believe that. And Triebel was one of those straight bureaucrats. Considering how many criminals have already been convicted, just because they had that inner urge to document everything.

But I digress. Actually, I just wanted to tell you that I kept my promise to get you out of the Triebel murder case. Otherwise, of course, my demand that you confess yourself to your deeds will be preserved.

Look for mails again tomorrow. Our game continues and it gets tougher. After all, you no longer have the good fairy who organized it all for you. Today I you have a day off. As far as my duties are concerned. You certainly want to see if everything is alright in your company."

MM couldn't help but read the mail several more times. The man had actually screwed him. During the telephone conversation, MM had actually offered only a return service if he were to get out of the suspicion of murder in the "Triebel" case. In fact, he had not thought of directly calling for a complete halt to blackmail.

So, he had to keep fighting the blackmailer. Luckily, he had now revealed that he could somehow observe MM in his house. There were means against this.

Two hours later, MM returned from his purchases. He hung all the walls with opaque fabric and set up radios throughout the house that would cover all the conversations he would have with permanent noise. That would cause enough problems for the blackmailer. Because the bugs and mini-cameras that were certainly hidden in the house were now almost useless. MM was sure of that.

Tuesday 24th May

Yvonne life in the small apartment became more and more boring. If she let it go comfortably, it might take her an hour in the morning to get dressed. After that, she had breakfast in peace and that was it. In the kitchen ended a kind of pneumatic post system. So far, she had found fresh bread rolls every morning. Presumably she would soon find fresh food here to cook something.

In this respect, she was actually doing pretty well for being a prisoner. The only thing she missed was that he would finally make contact with her. Except for the information sheets and the buns, she had not yet received any more signs. She was sure that would change immediately if, for example, she cut one of the robes. But she was also sure it wouldn't go down well for her. Still, she did not intent to monolog with the walls. Though she was sure that he would hear this about the undoubtedly installed bugs.

On the other hand, he was always quite communicative in the mails. Why not now? Maybe he had installed one of his puzzles for her. She just had to find it.

Over the next few hours, she systematically searched all the cupboards and rooms for hidden clues. At times, she felt like one of the brilliant detectives who do their job after telling the spectator 'I search the apartment. I don't know what I'm looking for, but the moment I see it, I'll know'.

In fact, there wasn't much to search. There were many books on the shelves. As a precaution, she looked behind every book, but found no hidden doors or compartments. Some cupboards were filled with social games. As with the books, nothing was hidden here. At least nothing obvious. There was nothing beyond that. Everything that made up a normal household, i.e. photo albums, reserve dishes, discarded winter clothes, all the little things that accumulate in the course of a lifetime and are not thrown away, were missing in the apartment.

Eventually, she gave up her search for the time being. To distract herself, she decided to turn on the TV for the first time since she was locked in the apartment.

Instead of showing some randomly chosen program, a little cartoon character jumped across the screen, announcing how much she was happy that the highly revered guest "Yvonne of MM-city" would give herself the honor to visit her the friendly Little Helper. Afterwards, Little Helper held up a sign asking Yvonne to either turn the TV off with the remote control or switch to the puzzle page.

On the puzzle page, Little Helper received her with a pair of nickel glasses on her nose and tried to give her voice a serious sound.

„It's nice that you want to pass the time with puzzles. The first puzzle to solve is the puzzle of the pin code for the free choice of program at the TV. Once you've found the code, you can simply enter it using the remote control. I will wait patiently.

Here is a small hint:

What you desire is hidden in this room.
The order of the scriptures is, it is hard to believe,
the key to the numbers,
and the end of the first puzzle torture is to be found

Please apologize for my inability to rhyme. Of course, I very much hope that the puzzle does not cause you any real torture, but I am only a little helper and therefore I couldn't think of a better lyrical text."

So that's what the kidnapper had in mind. She was supposed to solve puzzles and he would probably watch her. Really sick. But what else should she do? The concern that he would punish her - in whatever way - if she did not cooperate was simply too great. She knew nothing about him and therefore could not even foresee what he would do and what means he had to enforce his will.

164

So, she started to solve the puzzle. If the task wasn't designed to make her think outside the box, 'room' meant, first of all, simply the room in which she sat right now. By 'scriptures' on the other hand, either the Bible or the book collection that was on the shelves could be meant. Since there was no Bible on the shelves, she opted for the second variant. The task then, was to extract the solution from the order of the books on the shelves. If she didn't succeed, she had to try to see the clue as something encrypted.

***

MM had spent the whole morning picking up the old cases. A work that Triebel had already begun before his assassination. For MM, however, the cases revealed simply nothing. It was just a collection of incompetent businessmen who had been waiting to be bamboozled by someone like him. How could anyone be able to draw any conclusions from this?

By chance, he discovered a new mail on the computer.

„Dear MM, nice to see that you are able to perform complicated thought processes. Decorating the apartment with fabrics and the permanent acoustic irradiation: My respect. However, I would like to point out that this also puts you in a situation of constant nervous tension. This in turn, at least in my point of view, means that you will not be able to fight against me with the full possession of your brain capacity. In all modesty, however, I believe I can claim that this is the least you need to do. You do want to finish our little duel victorious? Don't you?

As I mention the word 'duel': You still don't have the free choice of weapons, or to put it more precisely: If you choose weapons that I dislike, I have the right to remove them from the game. Of course I don't want to bore you, but private detectives are among the banned weapons. Whereby these species is not as available as it was some days ago. At least according to my research.

165

Let's face your next task. I don't want to wrap it as one of the little puzzles I love so much. You're not smart enough to solve it. Here it comes:

From now on until Thursday midnight you are not allowed to leave the house. You won't receive a visit or communicate over the phone. This also means that you are not allowed to pick up the phone in the first place. Even if it should ring. As we're already talk about bells: When the doorbell is activated, you simply don't open the door.

I think you've understood the task?

Wishing that you have some contemplative days of inner contemplation ahead of you, I remain with kind greetings and the assurance that I will mail again on Friday"

The often he read the mail, the more he got into helpless anger. The blackmailer apparently had much more possibilities than MM could have imagined. He had to admit that he had not come any closer to the blackmailer in the whole days of the past. The man had killed two people without any scruples and, as he himself admitted in the mail, he had bugged and wired his entire house. MM couldn't even be sure if he could use the toilet unobserved. The only thing he knew immediately was that he certainly wouldn't be sitting in his house until midnight on Thursday. The only chance to defend himself was to go out and let down his net unobserved. After wasting time with old files all morning, this would be his next action. However, he had to wait for the night to hide himself in darkness, as the exits of his house were simply too easy to monitor at daylight.

***

Yvonne could not see any patterns in the arrangement of the books. After she had realized the task, she was happy for putting every book back in place in her search in the morning and not throwing them on a heap. It always had advantages when you had a well-developed sense of order. She had even considered whether to sort the books better. Not even the

166

books of the same author stood together. Fortunately, however, she had been able to control herself. After all, she didn't want to live like that very special TV detective, who always put everything in order everywhere and even sometimes seemed to forget the actual case.

Yvonne continued to look at the shelves. How could it actually happen that someone arranged books so chaotically? Didn't everyone have any order? By size, by themes, by authors, something. Maybe after the date of purchase?

The wannabe-poem clearly said that the order of the books was the key. So, the order or better sequence could be the key. She went through the books beginning with the top left. Even the first two books didn't fit together 'Sherlock Holmes' and the 'Ghosts' of Ibsen. Well, depending on the angle of view, Sherlock Holmes also had something ghostly. But Ibsen was a great author of a very different caliber than Doyle. At least she assumed that. To be honest she hadn't read a single word from Ibsen. The book cover gave her the information that it was a family drama in three acts. The next book was the 'The Name of the Rose'. She knew that. After all, the author was more a scientist, if she had this correctly in mind. In this respect, he perhaps suited Ibsen more. Still, Yvonne couldn't tell if she was on the right track to solve the puzzle.

The next book was by Hakan Nesser. Well. So, another thriller. She had already read some of them. Right next to it, however, someone she had never heard of. Alfred H. Unger.

If she had at least the Internet, she could have researched every author. But she didn't. As a result, she didn't need to solve what she had already made clear to herself. It was essential that she kept her thoughts under control. If she digressed after a few books, she could never reach her goal.

'Müller', playwright. Since she had never found any contact to his works, although it must have been very good. But crime novels were just more entertaining. Like the next one: 'Deon Meyer', crime thriller from South Africa. Then again something serious: 'Horst Ehmke', the retired German politician. Certainly, something state-forming. She pulled out the book and, to her surprise, discovered that it was a thriller. It began with the murder of a prostitute. Respect. In the end, even such people have to have some fun, in doing something that is not so directly related to the past professional life.

She recognized the next book by the spine. Harry Potter had also found its way into the library, followed by two crime writers Asa Larsson and Adler Olsen.

Where is all this supposed to lead?

***

At last the night had come. MM opened the basement door. There was nothing to hear. He carefully crept up the stairs and listened again into the night. Before entering the garden, he stopped again, waiting for his eyes to get used to the darkness. He was annoyed that he hadn't already done it in the basement. Just a few minutes without light and his eyes would already be at their maximum power. Now it seemed to take him an eternity to finally be able to recognize the outlines of the bushes and trees.

The sudden shrill alarm went through all his bones. At first, he thought it was the neighbors' alarm system. It was only when his heartbeat calmed down that he realized that the noise was coming from his own house. He had definitely turned off the alarm system. Nevertheless, his house raised the alarm. Ill-starred as he was, he would surely be arrested as a burglar if he ran away. He had no choice but to walk down the stairs again. While he tried to hold both ears with the upper arm and hand of his left arm, he frantically searched for the basement key with the other hand. The moment he opened the door and set out to find the source of the alarm, the spook was gone.

His ears still sent him a continuous tone and his head seemed to buzz, but the alarm was silent. After a short search, he found a small wire connected to the door. Apparently, it triggered the alarm via a small magnetic switch. All he had to do now was find and destroy the loudspeaker, so he could finally leave the house.

But before he could search, the doorbell rang. As he stepped into the hallway, he sensed a shadow moving quickly toward him. Before he could react, he was grabbed and pushed against the wall. A man held a service card in front of his nose.

„Domus Secur. We have been informed of the unauthorized opening of a door in this house. Can you identify yourself?"

„At most, I can identify you! You are two guys that do not belong to Germany! I'd like to help you to go back in your country! As soon as possible!"

In response, his arms, which were held entangled behind his back, were pushed a little higher, so that he had to involuntarily make a hollow back.

„Even if you do not like it, we are German citizens and we will now hand you over to the German authorities. Until they arrive, we are authorized to detain you."

In the device attached to his shoulder, he commanded „Team B. Call the cops. We have a burglar who cannot identify himself. Access via the cellar door."

Not the first time in these days MM had to fight down his anger and apologize.

„Now stay calm. That just slipped out. If you were so kind to reach into my left back pocket. There you will find my ID card. I don't know who hired you, but certainly it wasn't me. Nevertheless, this is my house and I therefore have the right to be here."

The spokesman took the ID card and compared the picture to MM.

„I don't see too much matchings. But I am ready to give you a chance. Describe the photo!"

„I know. I have long hair and not so many holes in my ears"

„And the rest of the data? Have you learned them by heart?"

MM gave him his name, place of birth and the other information that he thought had to be on an identity card.

„That is true so far. So, you insist that you are Mr. Müller?"

He already noticed that his blood got racing again.

„Of course, I insist and it's time for you to let me go."

To confirm, he jerked his arms, but this did not impress the firm grip of the man in any way.

„Can you please explain to me how the alarm was raised?"

„I have no idea. I wanted to go through the basement into the garden and that's when the thing started."

„Did you accidentally not turn off the alarm system?"

„Damn! I turned off the fucking alarm system. I have no idea how it could start! In addition, my alarm system reports very differently. Complete differently."

The longer the silence on this answer lasted, the clearer MM became that he risked his neck with careless talk.

„So, you claim to live here and but you don't know the alarm system that secures their own basement door? Did I understand that correctly?"

MM preferred not to give an answer. The tone of voice changed to a relaxed mode when the man continued.

„Okay, Mr. Müller. I'm sure you can take that little joke. From now on we'll be serious. I tell you what has happened here, Mr. Müller. You are up to your neck in serious problems and wanted to say goodbye by escaping from your house arrest. However, we have been hired to monitor this house arrest discreetly, but if it is necessary, we have the license to 'monitor' very assertively. That is what we have just done. Our service ends at exactly midnight on Thursday and be assured that we will do this service well, because I can inform you that we will receive an additional reward for every documented escape attempt."

Without thinking for a long time, MM fell into its long-practice, successful pattern of behavior.

„Whatever he pays, I double."

„We also receive a reward for every documented attempted bribery. I have to thank on behalf of the team."

MM would have preferred to hit the wall with his forehead.

„I notice that you have understood. Listen carefully Mr. Müller. My colleague will now let you go. After that we will leave the house in peace and move back into our positions."

MM nodded his head imperceptibly.

„I wish a good night's sleep."

Without letting him out of sight, the two retreated to the door and left the house.

Wednesday 25th May

In the middle of the night, Yvonne suddenly woke up. „The order of the scriptures!" That was quite simply the sequence without any thinking outside the box. She ran to the shelf and took note of the titles of the first books and the names of the authors. In the end, she had a list of 15 titles and authors. Everything that was on the top shelf.

First, she tried it with the initial letters of the titles with no result. She then wrote the authors' initial letters one after the other and received:

„DIENUMMERLAUTET" (translated thenumberis)

She looked briefly at the letters, and cheerfully raised her arms into the air „The number is" This could not really be a coincidence. She added the names of the next writers and finally got

„DIENUMMERLAUTETEINSNULLNULLNEUN"

So, the code was 1009. The riddle was solved.

Going back to bed was out of the question at the moment. She was far too awake to do so. So, she sat down again at the Little Helper and entered the number.

Little Helper grinned all over her face and applauded.

„Well done Yvonne. You have just reached the first level. You can now watch as much television as you want. But if you want to have a little puzzle again, then just press the pin code you discovered right now plus 1. Get the picture?"

Little Helper paused and looked attentively into the camera.

„If not, it's not bad either, as I'll tell you that every time you turn on the TV. Of course, without applause. I don't want to be a bore."

With that Little Helper disappeared and opened the choice of television channels. Yvonne went back to bed with a satisfied feeling. Actually strange, she thought, I'm a prisoner here but still satisfied.

***

MM could only dream of this. He still couldn't believe that he had been made a prisoner in his own house. There had to be some way to leave the house without the guards being able to prevent him from doing so. But how? For sure physical violence was not an option. These musclemen would carry him back to his house on the outstretched arm and tell him how much additional money he had just given them again. Help by phone was also not possible, as they sure were listening to all his phone calls. The same was certainly true for the mobile phone he had received from Yvonne. Nevertheless, there had to be a way. After all, there had always been a way in his life.

He spent the rest of the night restless walking through his house. He suspected that he was being watched through any sensors or hidden cameras, and that he was now showing that he was exactly in the state the blackmailer probably wanted to see him in, but he couldn't help it. After a few hours, he had at least calmed down to a level that allowed him to sit down.

The shrill of a doorbell stopped the little bit of sleep he had found in the armchair. He had trouble orienting himself at first, but then the memory of the previous night came over him faster than he had hoped. Again, the bell rang. It wasn't his doorbell and it didn't come out of that direction. He checked where the noise came from and found a mobile phone in the study.

„Yes?"

„Good morning MM."

Again, this disgusting synthetic voice.

„I don't want to annoy you by asking if you've had a pleasant night. I know that it was not pleasant and I am happy to confess that I am pleased with knowing that.

I think that my friends have been able to convince you that they will do their job with all the requested responsibly. They will watch over you until midnight tomorrow. You might have some hopes that this will be your big moment? That you will be master of your life again? I'm so sorry (laughter). I would like to point out to you that I'm already busy with arranging some more games for you. The end will only be reached with your self-denunciation. Perhaps also prematurely. They still did not connect you to Karlsson. Working with professionals once."

MM would have preferred to smash the mobile phone against the wall with all his might, but could still stop himself from doing so.

„You don't want to talk anymore? Well, then I just explain to you that of course I don't want to let you starve to death. So, if you want to leave the house for shopping, just go to the garage and wave to the camera above the garage door. I wish you a good day."

When MM wanted to set the breakfast table, he realized that he really didn't have much food anymore. He had always been convinced that there were masses of pizzas and the like in the freezer, that there was canned food in the kitchen drawers, and that there was a supply of pasta and rice in the house. But as much as he was searching, he couldn't find anything. Yvonne had apparently only shopped from day to day. She simply was a complete disappointment. He just got enough to have breakfast. When he thought of the previous day, he noticed that he had completely forgotten to eat. This meant that the blackmailers pressure made much more than he wanted to admit. With the end of breakfast, the last food disappeared in his stomach. From now on, therefore, hunger was the motto. Or... He put his hands on the temples to concentrate better. What if he found a way to escape during his 'parole'? The guards could badly control him in public and drag him away. The risk that someone would intervene or would trigger complications was far too great.

The following hour he tried to weigh all sorts of dangers and problems, but then came to the conclusion that as long as he would only make the escape attempt if he saw a really good chance, he would not take any risks. At worst, he would come back with a bag full of food. So: Just do it.

***

174

Yvonne had slept until she was awakened by the sun shining on her bed. After she had passed the usual dressing procedure, she sat comfortably at the table and read the morning newspaper during breakfast. As always, she had found everything in the 'tube-mail-system'. Afterwards, she sat down on the sofa as comfortably as it was possible with the corset and let Little Helper announce the next task.

„It's nice that you're looking for the next challenge. The first thing I want to assure you is that the reward will be of great value to you, because this time you will get fresh food. If you can't solve the task but still need fresh food, you can let me know at any time by entering this pin code."

She pointed to the four-digit code in the lower left edge of the screen.

„But I have to warn you, because it will make your life a little more uncomfortable." With a wave of her hand, she added „But what am I talking about? You would even manage the task whilst standing on your head."

After a short break Little Helper added.

„That was no hint. Just wanted to say that you can solve it without problems."

With a business face, she went to the side a little bit, so that the camera had to follow her. After a few steps, she stopped in front of a screen. She looked briefly into the camera, then took a remote control in her hand and had a picture appear on the screen. Yvonne could see a richly ornamented vase.

„Ornaments, dear Yvonne, are not actually images as we know them from great artists of contemporary history. Although they are colors applied with more or less attention to detail and thus actually pictures, we do not see them as pictures."

Little Helper paused and looked up with a wrinkled forehead.

„I have to be careful that I don't go into too much detail, otherwise I solve, the actual challenge though you have to solve it. That would be something."

After a short break, she continued.

„Ornaments are very special pictures. They don't want to tell a story. They just want to be there and make a small or even large area a bit more beautiful. Just as the piano player in the noble restaurant does not want to entertain anyone with his art, but simply wants to hide away the background silence."

She looked at the picture again and nodded approvingly, as if to praise herself for her remarks.

The next picture showed a Roman mosaic.

„Here we have the classical synthesis between image and ornamentation. I almost tend to call this metamorphosis. As you can see, the image is framed by one of the classic imaginative Roman ornaments. A line that bends at regular intervals by 90° and thus continues until it has returned to its beginning. Inside, however, a table society is depicted. What leads me to put this image in the realm of metamorphosis is the area above the head of the landlord."

She pointed the light pointer at the appropriate area.

„Here you can clearly see how the ornament is widening and slowly changing to a vine with juicy grapes."

Little Helper looked at the picture for a while with sincere respect and muttered again and again: „marvelous"

The following pictures showed ornaments from all possible countries and epochs. After half an hour, Little Helper finished her talk and turned again to Yvonne.

„Now your task: Find the four digits of the next code in the ornaments. To put the digits in the correct order, arrange them according to their length with the shortest starting."

She bowed gallantly and disappeared after saying goodbye and wishing Yvonne good luck.

If Yvonne would have looked in a mirror now, she would probably have seen only one big question mark in her face. She had not expected that she would have to remember all the ornaments in order to look for any digits hidden in them. She again chose the menu to see the task again.

„Hello Yvonne. I guess you want to see all the ornaments again. You can do this as many times as you like, but I want to be fair and point out that you won't solve the task in doing that."

Afterwards, the slideshow began.

***

No sooner had he waved into the camera when a voice came out of a small loudspeaker.

„Yes?"

Since MM did not know where the microphone was in which he had to speak, he continued to look into the camera.

„I need something to eat!"

„That is what we expected. Do you want to shop yourself or do you prefer to give us a shopping list?"

That's what they thought. But not with him. Not with MM.

„Of course, I go shopping myself! How can I know if you aren't putting any contaminated goods into the bag and then proudly get special points from your mad client?"

When after a little pause there was no answer, MM noticed how the anger about his helplessness came up again.

„Now you're opening this cursed gate and let me out of here!"

To confirm, he shook the small garage door that led into the garden. Finally, the voice answered.

„If you want to shop yourself, there is of course the possibility that we will lose sight contact by some stupid coincidence. You may be able to use this for an escape attempt. But that is not in the interest of our client. We must therefore take precautions to enable us to find you at any time. That is why I ask you again if you do not want to give us a shopping list."

„No, not at all. I'm gonna shop myself or I will starve! Let me out now!"

„Your arrest is only ordered until midnight tomorrow evening. You cannot starve to death in such a short time. Not by any stretch of imagination. All you can achieve during this time is to get the idea of hunger. An educated man like you should know that."

„Teach whom you want and what you want, but leave me alone with your stupid talk! I'm gonna shop now and you're going to stop these stupid discussions!"

„Ok. Please step back from the door. Two colleagues will now come in and explain how the shopping tour works."

MM stepped back a few steps. Two well-muscled men came through the door. At least they hadn't squeezed themselves into tight business suits. This always looked rather ridiculous. Stupid fighting machines will never become smarter by putting themselves in suits. One of them handed him a tightly printed note.

„Please read this and sign."

With that, he took a step back and went into waiting. MM had the impression that his counterpart was prepared to spend any length of time in this position. The note contained the terms and conditions of a personal surveillance company whose name he had never heard of. After reading the first paragraphs, he decided to skip the rest. After all, the same thing was always said in these treaty texts. Legal quibbles. He had already bamboozled some of his victims with papers like that. But these were the formulations that could be looked at in rough quantities in all sorts of contracts. Clearly no danger to him. So, he signed and handed the paper back to the muscle man. At the same moment something snapped around his neck. MM had not paid attention to the second man who had approached unnoticed behind his back. When he grabbed his neck, he felt a wide smooth collar.

„What did you do? Stupid idiots!"

„You have just agreed to be monitored by an electronic neck collar"

With the hint of a smile, he gave MM time to let it sink in. Then he added: „Of course, you will not be able to open this collar without the use of the appropriate key. I can only recommend that you do not try, as you could be seriously harmed."

178

MM scanned the collar. All he could feel was that it had a smooth surface. There was no lock. He ran into the house and looked in the mirror. He was wearing a wide stainless-steel collar. Back in the garage, he noticed that the door was open. His two guards stood in wait-and-see.

„Your perverted idiots probably don't think I'm going to the city looking like this?"

„The decision whether or not to buy the desired food is up to you. However, I would like to clarify the misunderstanding with 'driving'. Of course, you do not have a car or anything like that. You will have to walk."

MM could hardly bear the implicitness with which his counterpart thought he could decide what MM had to do and how.

„Listen. I don't care what your client says at all."

MM pointed to his car.

„I'm going to drive into the city with exactly that car. Then I will purchase something to eat. And you're not going to stop me. Have I made myself clear enough now?"

Instead of an answer, the two stepped aside and opened the way to the car. He should have treated these idiots like that from the beginning on. Such muscle-men always need one to give them clear commands. Then they are happy.

As he sat at the steering wheel of his luxury car, unexpected enthusiasm arose. He just had to start the engine, slowly slide out of the garage and the road would be his road to freedom.

He pressed the start-button and was abruptly ripped out of his dreams. The immobilizer was activated. The display informed him that a key had been detected but it had the wrong encoding. Another attempt would inevitably lead to an alarm.

MM stared at the display in disbelief. How could that happen? You can't just teach the system a new key coding. He pulled his car key out of his pocket. It looked like it always did. Especially the small scratch was still there. It was his key! No copy! He had no glue how they could manipulate the system.

A glance in the rear-traffic mirror showed him that the two were still standing at the driveway, waiting patiently for him.

If only they had laughed ugly. That would have been easier to work with than this controlled waiting-position and this noble, professional behavior.

He breathed three times deep in and out. Then he slowly got out and went to the two muscle-men. He had to put a good face on the matter.

***

Beatrice had taken up posts an hour ago. She was later than planned, as she was apparently not the only one who wanted to watch MMs house. The high-class VW minibus immediately caught her eye. Dark, almost black windows in a vehicle that was not in one of the many huge driveways were simply too conspicuous in such a noble residential area. Unaware of whether she had already been seen, she had continued her walk at low pace and then approached the house in what she hoped was a sufficiently large radius from behind. There she found a small path that led past MMs garden door. Via the neighboring property that was completely covered with bushes, she was able to sneak up to the front of MMs house. So, she had witnessed the conversations and the collar-moment. In her judgement an extremely stylish collar. As Yvonne had described MM, his blood was probably boiling. When she saw that after an unimpressive attempt of intimidation, he was not able to start his car, she would have preferred to laugh out loud. Serves him right. His wife hadn't been there for days and he had nothing better to do than get harassed by the two beefcakes. Instead he should have asked the police to search for his wife.

Now he came out of the garage again and had to ask the two of them how he should buy his food without a car. The answer did not seem to please him. She saw his hands cramping. He made a few more attempts to dissuade the two from their proposal. Eventually everyone went to the minibus together and he was sent off with a large braided shopping basket. If Beatrice wasn't wrong, he had at least two or three kilometers to the next shop. You couldn't have everything. Super house in super area meant that the nearest shops couldn't be around the corner, because it wouldn't have been a super area anymore.

She cautiously withdrew from her post. Maybe she could still watch him shopping. Shortly after she left the small path, however, her attempt was interrupted. Her old colleague Rednich stopped next to her in his car.

„Hello Günther, nice to see that you stick to him. Is there any news?"

„Still the old Beatrice. You don't think I'm serving you our results now? Just out of old, collegial friendship?"

Beatrice had to smile.

„No. Of course not. But I can try my luck, don't I?"

She leaned down to the car and greeted Rednich's colleague, who was driving the car.

„I suppose you know MM is in serious trouble? His house is supervised by high-tech freelancers. It seems to me that he is not able to defend himself against these guys."

„And from this you conclude that his wife was kidnapped? MM is still in your focus because of his wife. Am I right?"

„Of course, you are right. If Yvonne's sayings about him are somewhat true, then I say: He can have as many problems as he wants. The more the better."

With a sympathetic grin, she added

„I can say that now. Do you have any idea what could have happened to his wife?"

Rednich looked briefly to Smidt, who signaled her approval with a nod.

„We have nothing to tackle. His house is bugged. Not by us. Nevertheless, this is quite handy. Our young people are very skilled in those things. He is fighting with the back to the wall. And as far as we can see it, he has no joker in the backhand. But his wife definitely is not here. Looks more like she's disappeared to a safe place."

„Thank you. I owe you something"

„You have my number. Inform me if you discover something and please inform me in any case when you hear something from his wife."

„Deal. But it may be the case that I can't reveal anything. After all, I'm alone and I don't want to make the mistake of underestimating the two guys who watch him."

„That is a reasonable intention. To support you in this, I suggest to remove the camouflage herb from your hair."

There again was this sympathetic smile that had always distinguished him so much.

As she twisted the little branch that had become entangled in her hair between her fingers, she pondered whether it would still be worth watching MM while shopping. She decided against it. The risk to observe in sight wasn't it worth.

***

MM hasn't been in a corner shop since childhood. He entered the shop with a consensual ringing of small cowbells, that were attached to the doorframe. The woman at the checkout and a man who arranged drugstore items ceased work. After a short hesitation the man moved to MM.

„Can I be of any help?"

He was unable to keep eye contact. He kept slipping down to the collar.

„I need something to eat."

„You've come to the right place."

With a conspiratorial smile, he bent a little closer to MM.

„Let me guess. Your wife is on tour with her friends and hasn't filled up the fridge?"

„Hubert!" The woman had meanwhile joined. „You can't ask our new customer such intimate questions!"

„Yes, I can. You just heard it, beloved Rosa."

His wife - 'Rosa' as MM learned – rolled her eyes and asked what MM would like.

„There, you see? Whenever I'm polite to the customers she rolls her eyes."

Hubert turned to MM for help, who didn't know what to think of the two of them.

„What exactly are you looking for?" Rosa wanted to know. Instead of MM, her husband answered.

„You have to offer something directly to the customer. Make suggestions. He may want bread. So, you have to make him aware of the different types of bread we can offer."

He turned back to MM and asked him to apologize for his wife's incompetence. To much for MM and for the moment. He had to intervene.

„I don't have to apologize at all. You are the service provider and I am the customer. Consequently, you have to follow my wishes and you do not have the right at all in my presence to rule your wife."

He would have better held his tongue. Hubert and Rosa looked at him aghast. While Rosa put her hands in her hips and fixed MM with a serious face, Hubert built up in front of him and declared with a firm voice:

„In my entire thirty years as an honorable retail salesman, I have not yet experienced such a thing. What customers think they can afford these days!"

He looked at Rosa.

„If you want to serve the gentleman, you are free to do so, otherwise" he turned his gaze to MM „I would ask you to leave our shop right away."

„I'll see what I can do" answered Rosa with hands still in her hips.

She threw a glance after her Hubert, who went to the back of the store

„So, what can I do for you?" Rosa wanted to know.

„There is nothing left. So, I need breakfast, lunch and dinner."

„That's a clear task. Well, we're going to do that."

While Rosa was serving him, he was under observation of Hubert, who pretended to deal with some important things in the back of the shop. A quarter of an hour later, MM left the store with a brimful filled shopping basket.

Thursday 26th May

Yvonne had spent the entire past day scanning the books for some passages to take her further in her search for ornaments. There was simply nothing to find.

As she stood in front of the mirror to pull on the corset, she pondered how she could continue the search. While she pulled the lace-up tight once more, her eyes fell on her forearms, on which the henna tattoo was still clearly visible. Part of the decoration looked like a Roman „I".

Of course. How could she come up with the idea of finding a random hit in the books? Time would not have been enough for this. The solution had to be much simpler. And the fact that the numbers were simply hidden in her tattoo was certainly one of the simplest solutions. After all, these were ornaments. She dressed calmly, had breakfast with a happy smile on her face, and then set about looking for the numbers on her hands and forearms.

***

„Good morning MM."

He couldn't hear the artificial voice without becoming aggressive. But he had to wait for what would happen.

„Don't you want to say 'good morning' my dear MM?"

So, what did he come up with again? Did the blackmailer have to make it clear to him at every opportunity that MM was ill-equipped to fight against him? MM decided to continue to wait.

„Too bad actually. After you made your way so bravely to the corner shop yesterday, I was in a generous mood for a little moment. I don't want to tell you what your price would have been. Your life is hard enough."

MM continued to listen to him in silence. As if he had actually received a reward. The guy just wanted to pull his leg.

„You are quite the great silent minority today! I don't know you like that. You're sick in the end? Fever? Something like that? Do I have to start a doctor-game?"

Silence.

„When I think about it that way, it's actually a very attractive relaxation exercise. Since I would appoint the doctor, of course you would not know whether he is a real doctor or not. In this respect, every examination and, above all, every medication would have a very special appeal."

That was enough for MM

„What is the reason for the call? Get to the point!"

„Oh, he can speak and he is also trying to take control. Of course, such qualities are not as easy to strip off as a dirty shirt. Doesn't matter. You asked a question and I want to answer it: I called to ask about your well-being. That's all. The current game lasts until midnight. There is nothing more to tell you about that.

No, wait. There was something else: Please don't come up with the idea of leaving the house right after the end of the game, because the next game starts midnight. You will find the rules tomorrow morning. Would 9 o'clock be okay? Then there would be plenty of time for breakfast. I'm not a monster. Now that you've shopped so nicely."

Did the guy really think he could go on with it forever? The muscle-packed idiots hadn't taken his collar off yesterday, although that was part of the deal. Instead, they had said something about 'Contract not properly read'. What he needed first was a reliable and discreet man to help him getting rid of this terrible collar. He had no choice but to try his luck.

***

She had found the "I", the "XCI" and the "VIII". There was definitely no more. Translated, these were in any case the 1 and the 8. However, the "XCI" caused her problems. "X" means 10 and "C" is 100. That much was clear to her. So "XC" could be 90. So "XCI" could be 91. Actually, quite conclusive even if she herself would have written "XIC" for 91. On the other hand, this could have been interpreted as 100-11, i.e. 89. In this respect, "XCI" was actually clearer.

So, she had the next four digits together. Now it was all about the order. 'To put the digits in the correct order, arrange them according to their length with the shortest starting' Little Helper had said. By the length could actually only mean the original Roman spelling. As a result, "I", "XCI" and "VIII" and thus the code "1918". The end of First World War, she immediately thought.

After entering the code, Little Helper greeted her sitting behind a desk. She had her head rested on one hand as she drummed bored on the table with the fingers of the other hand. After a short time, she pretended to have noticed Yvonne just in that moment.

„I thought I'd have to watch you scroll through books for another whole day. I'm happy that you had the idea to have a closer look on this wonderful henna-ornaments. Of course, 1918 is the correct code."

Little Helper rose and made a deep respectful bow.

„As promised, you will be equipped with fresh goods in these minutes. This should actually be enough for the moment. I need a bit of preparation for the next task. It is up to you what you will do with this day. See you!"

***

What should he do with all the information about the locksmiths? How could the Internet supposedly be so helpful when he received everything indiscriminately distributed across his country under the entry locksmith in response? He was also not interested in the fact that after a whole week, some former locksmith in the 19th century had not found a procedure to open a newly developed lock without the appropriate key. He just wanted to know if there was a discreet and capable locksmith somewhere in his neighborhood.

He tried it with 'discreet locksmith'. Why did the great Internet now bring him job ads and a script for discrete math? Didn't the internet know the difference between 'discreet' and 'discrete'? MM was about to smash the laptop into the corner.

To calm down, he decided to have a coffee. He had to keep himself under control. No matter what would happen. But how could he stay calm, when time was running short. His company would very soon go bust. He was the man to lead the company and take care. Nobody else.

When he returned with the coffee, there was a message at the bottom of the screen.

„You have a new mail: Breakout-proof closure..."

He opened the e-mail program and found a new mail.

Dear MM,

as I see to my delight, you are slowly becoming familiar with the world of the internet. The search terms you entered suggest that you are looking for a solution regarding the stylish collar that you voluntarily offered to wear since yesterday. Now I have to inform you that this collar can only be opened with the right key or very well-founded knowledge of its construction. If you do something wrong, it can lead to many undesirable effects. One of these is that a small tank will be destroyed. A tank with the second part of a two-component adhesive. Do I have to be more precise? Yes? I'd be glad to. The adhesive takes about an hour to cure. By the way, you can speed this up by heat. After curing, the closure is sealed. That you don't get it wrong: If this has happened, I can throw the key into a deep lake or hand it over to you. It doesn't matter, because it's just worthless. The lock is then a rock-hard mass.

It took a lot of attempts, but finally a well-done masterpiece. Unfortunately, not mine. So, I am not allowed to praise myself.

But now to the important things of life. I had promised to play another game with you. The game is called 'Life at the bottom'. Since you seem to be bored, we start with it right now. You don't have to wait for midnight. That's good news. Isn't it? You will certainly be happy, as you are finally allowed to get out again. To put it in concrete terms, you have half an hour to leave your house from now on. Expect your return

Sunday night. Until then, you can essentially do what you want as long as you don't enter buildings.

I stay with the best wishes for the rest of the day and hope you have a lot of fun with the little game."

MM read the mail a few more times and noticed with each time that he again became more and more frustrated about the hopelessness of his situation.

Did the man never make a mistake? Everyone makes mistakes. Especially those who liked to hear themselves talking. So why not the blackmailer? MM tried, as best he could, to recapitulate everything that had happened in the past few weeks.

Everything he did in his house; the blackmailer could see and hear. Presumably he had already installed the bugs when he cracked the safe. Still, he couldn't have foreseen everything that happened so accurately. So, it was inevitable that he or his henchmen had made even more visits to his house, for example to prepare the basement door with the alarm system.

What did this realization bring him to solve his problem? He didn't know. Why could the heroes in the crime novels always begin to solve the problem on the basis of such a realization? Easy. Because the bad guy was always looking for physical closeness to the victim.

Exactly that was the problem. The blackmailer had all the cards in his hand. He could hand him over to the police at any time. And he obviously had no interest in being near him.

It was also clear that he would never stop playing his games. There was no reason to hope that he would stop in the near future. He would never look for a new victim because he definitely had some very personal reasons.

As a result, MM could only stop the whole thing by voluntary declaration or he had to find the blackmailer and eliminate him.

The first possibility was out of the question. So how could he really get close to the blackmailer?

His computer got a new mail

„Dear MM,

we both know that I am well aware of your movements within your luxury building. In this respect, I know that you have read the last mail. Now I have the idea that you want to rebel a little bit against the rules of the new game. As with a small child who consciously or unconsciously tests its limits with his disobedience, I must insist on compliance with the rules. So please be a good boy and leave the house immediately."

MM smiled. In fact, this was an unwanted through ball. What could the blackmailer do? He would again threaten to publish the documents. But would he really do that? At that very moment, he would irrevocably give up his leadership. He would no longer have any influence on what would happen next.

That was the card MM had to play now. MM began the inspection in the living room. He pushed every piece of furniture aside and turned every book. Somewhere the little bugs had to be hidden. Since he had no idea to leave the house in the near future, he forced himself to work slowly and carefully. In fact, after a few hours, he had found three suspicious items in his living room, which he immediately destroyed with a hammer before he threw them in the garbage. He hoped that the blackmailer would sit somewhere and have a small painful explosion in his ear canals with every hammer stroke.

When it rang at the door, he saw that his guards had returned. Instead of opening, MM continued the search. He took the fact that the guards left his property after a short time with a certain satisfaction, but he was also aware that he was far from winning. They would, of course, try to enter his house and then force him out of the house. He couldn't do more than block the basement door from the inside. He couldn't possibly secure all the windows. Since it was not assumed that they would gain violent access to his house during the day, he could feel reasonably safe until the evening.

With new energy, he again searched for bugs.

***

Beatrice had settled in the park again with Rondo. The windows of MMs house were still darkened. It almost seemed as if MM wanted to isolate himself. After Beatrice could not see the guards in the morning, they now had returned to their position. They had changed the car, but were still conspicuous enough. At least for Beatrice.

But nevertheless, she could stare at the house as long as she wanted. Nothing happened.

Apparently, the guards in the mini bus although waited for something to happen. Again and again, one of them got out to smoke a cigarette. Real professional, Beatrice thought derogatorily. No trace of camouflage. But maybe they didn't want to hide from MM. The whole thing looked more like the tactic 'Look! Here I stand and I'm watching you'. But what should all this be for?

Just when she wanted to propose to Rondo to stop it for the moment, MM came to the door. Instead of leaving, he took the garden hose out of the garage and started watering the garden. Immediately two of the guards came out of the mini bus. He looked forward to them. When they were close enough, he pointed the hose at them and sprayed them wet. At the same time, he screamed that they had to leave his property.

Beatrice couldn't believe that this really happened. Presumably the guys were equipped with deadly weapons and MM couldn't think of anything better than spraying them wet with the garden hose. Since it was still daylight and enough passersby were witnesses, the guards had no option but to go back to their mini bus. A short time later, they drove off.

Beatrice had actually expected MM to leave the house now, but nothing happened. When Rondo suggested taking the opportunity and running over quickly, Beatrice showed him another suspicious car.

190

„If we get into the firing line, it could be really dangerous."

Eventually, they took their things and strolled to the other side of the park, where they had parked their car. Just before they got there, a cyclist approached from behind. When Beatrice turned briefly to see which side he wanted to pass on, she was surprised to see MM. As he fixed her, he seemed to have searched for and found Beatrice.

„Finally got you, slut!"

Beatrice noticed Rondo's hand stretching.

„Me?"

MM looked around demonstratively.

„I don't see anyone else here."

Beatrice looked at him waiting. She didn't had a really good idea, why he called her 'slut', but he would certainly explain it to her.

„Do you think I don't realize you're hanging around in front of my house with your weird dude all the time? So, tell me. Now that I'm facing you directly and you don't have any of your powerful friends with you. How long should the game last?"

„What game do you mean?"

The redness of anger in his face indicated that he did not take it for true.

„You have been blackmailing me for a few weeks with some obscure documents and we will put an end to this now and here! As you noticed today, I will no longer play the fool for your amusement."

„Oh, that's what you mean. Unfortunately, I have to disappoint you. I know what you are talking about, but I know it only because Yvonne and me became friends in the last few weeks. And she told me about these strange city tours. So, I am in front of your house because I am trying to find a trace of Yvonne. It almost seems to me that I am the only one who is worried about Yvonne. What do you know about her whereabouts?"

With a hint of uncertainty in the voice, MM answered:

„Nothing. She just cut it off and left me alone with my problems. In this respect, she can stay where she is. Wherever she is."

Now that Beatrice spoke directly to MM for the first time, she couldn't understand how Yvonne could stand by his side for so long. He was even more cold than she had suspected.

„Let's say she's in the hands of the blackmailer. You're not afraid that he might do anything to her? Chic collar by the way." She took a closer look. „I don't even know the brand. Where did you get that from?"

„You can't care less about that?"

„After all, I have often freed people from such things. In this respect, I am always interested when I see one that I do not yet know."

She could see hope flashing in his eyes.

„Do you think you can open this?"

„I don't know. If you would have listened carefully, you wouldn't have missed the fact that I do not know the brand."

„Well. If you make it, I will forget the blackmail thing. After that, the two of us can continue our daily business undisturbed."

„Sorry?" Beatrice could not and did not want to follow his thoughts. „I am not the blackmailer. I already said that. What is the point of the text that you have just produced? If I open the collar, or at least try to do so, it is certainly not because I want to help you. That would be simply out of a professional interest. After all, you have just insulted me in the worst possible way. Already forgotten?"

MM looked at her perplexed and had to clear his throat before he could ask her:

„Will you give it a try or not?"

„If I try to do that, I need my tools and keys. Best of all, you'll come to my store tomorrow."

When Beatrice was looking for a business card, his gaze went over her shoulder to the parking lot. MMs eyes opened for a moment as if he had recognized someone he didn't want to meet. Without further explanation, he turned his bike and disappeared towards the park.

Rondo looked after him.

„What was that?"

„MM in full bloom. Strange. I didn't expect that he would stop the conversation so quickly. I was sure I could get him in my shop."

Beatrice was disappointed as she let the card disappear in her pocket.

„It seemed to me that he had seen something. There was such a brief flash in his eyes. Maybe something in the parking lot." Rondo suspected.

Beatrice could not see anything conspicuous. Actually, she had been expecting the mini bus. But nothing of the sort was visible. An older man who had just returned from his walk was the only person she could see.

„We are doing a little tour with an unknown destination. First, we walk to the parking lot. Slowly."

Rondo looked at her.

„What did I miss? Actually, I thought that we would cook delicious food now and enjoy the rest of the day. You don't want to follow this grandpa?"

„Just chase him. But keep your distance. If we lose him, we lose him. In any case, think of the following: If he is the wanted person, then he will be very observant. Any car with conspicuous overtaking maneuvers will be suspicious for him. So, better lose him than fetch his interest. I've already noted the license plate anyway."

Rondo rolled his eyes.

„I understood. You give me the lecture every time we are in such a situation."

Friday 27ᵗʰ May

When she opened the door in the morning, she found a box together with a piece of paper.

„*Dear Yvonne, unfortunately, since yesterday new conditions have occurred which make it impossible for me to continue the little game with you, though I really enjoyed it. So, when you open this box you will find the clothes you wore, as your dear MM decided to leave you to my hands. Yes, that is the truth. He did it just to regain his miserable little freedom.*"

Yvonne sat on the lid of the box and read the lines again. But the words remained the same.

„*Probably you won't really want to believe me. Yes, you'll think MM has been pretty much off the track lately, but he would never do anything like that. You can find a small proof in the box. Play the old-fashioned MP3 player and then think about it in peace. I sincerely swear that this is an original recording.*

For my part, I have to say goodbye to you now. Other tasks call me. Farewell.

PS.: That shouldn't sound arrogant, but somehow I have to put it. Please finally grow up and live your own life. You deserve it."

Yvonne ripped open the box and started the player. She heard MMs voice.

„*If it's not the money, what can I do to be whitewash myself from the murder suspect? There must be a solution. Say it and I will do it as far as it is in my power.*"

After a long pause, a strange synthetic voice gave the answer.

„*Well, there would indeed be an alternative. Deliver Yvonne out to my hands and we have a deal.*"

„*What do you have in mind for her now? She is so proud to behave so well. She's always been keen to go along with all the shit you asked her to do. Is that no longer enough for you?*"

Without waiting for an answer, MM continued.

194

„I'll go along with that. She's not the youngest anymore and lately quite rebellious. It won't be a problem to find someone new. What shall I do?"

After a short dwell time, which Yvonne needed to recover somewhat from the shock, the artificial voice gave the answer.

„Ask her to join you at the forest parking lot that you used frequently in the past. I would say 1 p.m. would have been very convenient for me."

With each time she played the phone call, her anger rose. Of course, in the last few days she had not behaved like the stupid little sweetheart that exists to be shown. But that probably didn't justify him being able to release her for kidnapping.

A short time later, she stood dressed in front of the house where she had spent the last days as a prisoner. The house stood completely lonely in the middle of a large arable area. Probably it had been a small farmhouse. In this case, the barns were missing, but... She interrupted her thoughts. After all, she wasn't here to think about the house, but to get back to MM as quickly as possible, give him a tongue-lashing and tell him that she would sue for a divorce.

Since there was no alternative anyway, she followed the only road. At some point she would arrive in some village and then eventually get the orientation where she was and how she could get back to her city.

Enough time in any case to think about how she wanted to continue. Maybe it didn't make much sense to run straight to MM. Eventually, he was under suspicion of murder, according to the phone call. Who guaranteed that he would not give her away to the highest bidder at the next opportunity? He did it once. So, he would certainly do it a second time.

After some time, she was so immersed in her thoughts that she only saw the old tractor approaching on a dirt road, despite its rattling, at the last moment. In the seat sat a young man with a beret and a cigarette in the corner of his mouth. She couldn't have imagined a Frenchman better

„Attention Madam!"

Yvonne looked at the man in confusion.

195

„Am I in France?"

When she received only a slightly amused look, she asked „France?" afterward.

„Bien sûr. C'est la France."

The man looked at her, grinning broadly, expectantly. Since Yvonne had never learned French, she could only hope that he understood her language.

„Do you speak my language?"

„Yes, I do. I would prefer the regional dialect but I take it for sure that you wouldn't understand a single word."

Again, he was waiting for her answer.

„I've lost of orientation. A bit. Where am I now?"

„In the Eifel. At least about."

„Ah. Eifel, then. How do I get away from here?"

He pointed to the street.

„Always follow the street and look for signs that read like references to big cities."

Yvonne looked at him with anticipation. More text had to come out of this man by itself. But he was again sitting expectantly on his tractor. Lack of time did not seem to exist for him.

„That would be, for example?" Yvonne pondered where she could find the Eifel at the German map. „Cologne?"

„Maybe"

„Can't you just tell me where I am and how to get away from here?"

For a moment, he looked down the street again. But then he seemed to think of something better.

„Let's see. Don't you really know where you are now or is this a weird big-city mess to fool little farmers like me?"

„It's a bit complicated and when I tell the whole story it's probably going to take a bit of time and in the end, you don't believe me anyway what I'm telling you. That's really a bit... surreal."

„Surreal. So it is. All right. Therefore. I'll make a 'real' offer. You jump here on this 'real' hard seat and I take you to the next village. If you are lucky, you will catch the morning bus, which will take you to the nearest Eifel metropolis. From there you can travel by public transport to even larger cities such as Cologne."

„Wow. These were a few sentences at a time and also constructively."

Yvonne climbed onto the wooden seat, which was on one of the rear wheels.

„Constructive, surreal" she heard him muttering shaking his head as he got the tractor back on its way.

After some time spent silently behind the steering wheel, he turned to Yvonne.

„To be a little serious now. What are you really doing here? When I think about which direction you came from, there is actually only one house..."

„And you want to know if I'm coming from there?"

Yvonne answered after he nodded.

„Yes, I come from there. Is this something special?"

Only now did he look at her more closely. He saw both her collar and henna tattoos on her hands.

„Oh man. Why doesn't this surprise me?"

„Explain it to me. Here in the village, the house might be a topic of conversation. What are they telling themselves?"

„Well, girl, if you don't know what to tell about the house and its crazy occupants, then I don't know what to tell you. Because otherwise you would know that after all."

„Sorry?"

He looked at her with a laugh.

„Have I assembled one of my complicated sentences again?" Without waiting for an answer, he continued. „What I meant is that there can only be rumors in the village. But if you've been in it, you should know what's going on. So why are you curious about rumors?"

„For example, I would like to know who owns the house in the first place."

„You probably know who invited you there."

Yvonne wasn't sure how much she really wanted to tell. After all, she got to know the man just since a few minutes.

„Who are you? I think we just completely forgot to introduce ourselves. In any case, I'm Yvonne."

„Jacques."

Again, he looked at her expectantly.

„French?"

„My mother had some preference for France. That's why I have the name."

„And? You're often in France?"

„No. I never learned the language to my mother's chagrin, and I don't like going on holiday in a country where I don't understand the national language. As a child, of course, I was there many times. But no more as an adult."

„Ah. I understand. That is, of course, true. It's always stupid when you can't understand people. Especially since the French probably don't really like to speak other languages. As I have heard."

„Yes. I think that's the way it is."

By now they had arrived in the village. He stopped at the bus stop and studied the timetable.

„You've been unlucky now. The next connection would be tonight."

„And how do I get away now?"

„By hitchhike or tonight."

Only now did Yvonne take a closer look around her

„This is completely deserted here. Not a single person can be seen."

„As you say that. Yes, I think that is the case."

He pulled up his shoulders apologetically.

„We are just too far away for normal working people. Such villages are doomed to fail in modern times."

„And how should I get away with hitchhiking?"

„Probably not at all," he grinned at her. „Was probably a little joke of mine."

„Ah. Well, great."

She descended from the tractor.

„Thank you anyway for the short lift to this wonderful village."

„But I can also offer you a connecting lift. However, it only goes a few corners further to my modest home. After all, you'll get a coffee for free."

Before she would stand around in a lifeless village, that was definitely the more entertaining alternative. So, she rose again.

A short time later, she followed him to his farm in between some lifeless terraced houses. He led her into the kitchen.

„Sit down. I'll be right back." As he walked out, he suggested „If you want, you can also start off the coffee maker."

„What are you actually doing here in this dying village?"

„Drinking coffee with unexpected guests."

„Very original. But now seriously. Are you the last farmer here? According to the motto: Someone has to hold the position?"

„Kind of. Actually, I only do this for fun. In reality, I am an artist."

Yvonne raised her eyebrow in amazement.

„What are you doing? Pictures?"

He put his cup down.

„I can show you. My studio is right next door."

„Why not?"

„If you want to follow me please Madame?"

He guided her through a few rooms and eventually stopped in front of a double door. He turned around with a gallant bow and pointed to the door.

„After you Madame. If you want to open the two door wings at the same time, my art will show itself at its best."

Yvonne tried it giggling with a courtly curtsy and pushed both door-handles down. Cause the two doors were difficult to be pushed open, she wanted to point out to him that this would be bad for the overall impression.

At the same moment, she noticed something hooked on her collar and pushed her into the studio with power. When she wanted to complain to Jacques, it was already too late. She noticed her being pulled up at the neck and heard a racy chain at the same time. The rattle only stopped when she stood on tiptoes and desperately tried to loosen the chain from her collar.

„I am a bondage artist and to make it clear right from the start. I am a bad guy, as I prefer to work with models that don't want to do it."

Yvonne was still far too busy finding her balance and keeping her breathing going. Since she was not exactly under the chain, her torso was too unstable. It was only when she held on to the chain with her hands over her head that she managed to stabilize her position. She quickly realized that he had been waiting for this, as at the same moment handcuffs were snapped, which tied her hands firmly to the chain.

Jacques took a step back and inspected his prey.

„Then I want to think about what I will do with you. Be sure that the next few hours won't be boring for you."

Finally, Yvonne could start to argue.

„What are you doing? Set me free immediately!"

He looked at her with regret.

„I was expecting more. At least a bit of hysterical screaming or something. Then I could have put a gag in your mouth to explain to you in peace that screaming is of no use, as the village, you saw it by yourself, is desert. The reason for the gag would have been simply that I can't bear the screaming. But now we can do it without a gag."

He left the room.

„What is to happen now? You get a kick to do what you do with helpless women?" she called.

„I just get the gag and then you'll notice what's happening" he called back from one of the adjoining rooms. Yvonne could hear him opening various drawers.

„Here it is. Beautifully designed and of course clean. Then open your mouth."

„Never. You're such a stupid idiot."

He broke into a smile.

„Well, wonderful. Now you start to fight back and do stupid things. I like it."

When he held her nose, Yvonne voluntarily opened her mouth. She had no other chance anyway.

„Good girl. Then I want to start the first session."

With these words he pulled up a table on which lay various neatly rolled up ropes.

***

The case MM was looking for was several years ago. It must have been one of his first acquisitions. The father of the company owner had even come to MM in person at the time to pull the cart out of the dirt for his son with a touching story of pledged pension. MM didn't quite get that together anymore. Of course, he had not been able to take care of the man's personal problems, when the deal had gone so perfectly up to that point. Perhaps the father had in fact given away all the guarantees on which he had built his retirement age. All just for his son. With the unfriendly takeover by MM everything was lost for the father. In all these years MM had not understood how people could be so stupid. In the end, however, his wealth was based on it, so he was glad that they existed.

MM has been searching the documents for far too long. He was sure that he had filed the case properly away. Just as he had done with all the acquisitions. Still, he couldn't find it. Eventually, he had to admit that the case was not in his file room. The files had to have been stolen during the burglary, that had started everything. He had briefly thought of his file basement on the night of the burglary, but since files were not interesting for burglars, he had assumed that the burglar had not touched them. As it now turned out, he wouldn't have noticed anything if he had looked up.

He had a significant problem with that. There were no copies. So, he had to go out himself and pick up the trace. But that did not work in his present state. First of all he had to be able to get rid of the collar so that he could finally act like a reasonable person again. If only he had asked this stupid bitch from the park for her address. On the other hand, he could not be sure that it was not yet another trap of the blackmailer. After all, Yvonne hadn't talked about a new girlfriend.

He could not assume that she would show up again voluntarily in front of his house. All he had to hope was to find a clue in Yvonne's stuff that would take him further.

At least he had found what he was looking for. A shop in the city. Presumably that was the place where Yvonne had bought the disgusting things for Luxembourg and all the other cities. He had no choice but to drive to the shop and let himself be helped by this Beatrice. A glance out of the window showed him that his guards still weren't back on their position. So, he had to take advantage of it. The only means of transport that was still available to him was the old bicycle. For sure, bicycles had only been invented for people who were too poor to go to the gym, but now he had no choice.

When he came to Beatrice shop, he had the impression that all eyes were only on him. The woman from the park could not be seen, but the woman at the checkout gave him hope that she would get in today.

„She has been too preoccupied with some private problems the last days. As one can hear, this has something to do with our sales attraction in recent weeks."

MM looked around

„What can be called a sales attraction in such a shop?"

„Well our new cleaning lady, who always wore some clothes from our offer when cleaning. This has boosted sales enormously."

„You let your cleaning staff work during opening hours, clothed with...", he was looking for the right word.

„Latex" the saleswoman helped out. He nodded approvingly.

He noticed how his intention to behave politely disappeared after the few sentences he had exchanged with the woman. What sick ideas could people come up with?

„Can I help you or would you like to wait for the boss in any case?" Before MM could give an answer, she continued. „We also have a nice selection of stainless-steel cuffs for wrists and ankles."

How could the woman seriously believe that such a thing might interest him? In addition, she looked at him so helpful. MM didn't know how to behave. He would have preferred to leave the store immediately. On the other hand, he absolutely needed this Beatrice so that his stupid collar finally could be taken off.

„No, I prefer to wait for the boss." Unconsciously, he grabbed the collar.

„I understand."

„I do not know what you are trying to understand. All I've said is that I want to wait for the boss."

„You look like one of those who have mislaid the key to their toy. But don't worry. Beatrice is good at such things. I have rarely experienced that she couldn't open a lock."

MM just wanted to be freed from the collar as quickly as possible. He had no intent to talk to any people who didn't see any problems in that.

„I make a suggestion. You look around the store a little bit and I call the boss and tell her, that she has a private client."

With a joyful smile, she reached for the phone.

„Beatrice also receives private customers? I didn't know that. What does she do to them?"

When MM turned to the owner of the voice, he faced a man with unkempt appearance. He was lustful-looking and somewhere in the mid-fifties. Since the saleswoman was already busy with the phone, the man turned all his attention to MM, who immediately gave him an answer with which he wanted to silence him.

„I don't know why I should give you any answer. This is an extremely private matter."

The moment the man's eyes grew, MM knew that he should not have used the phrase 'private matter'. The man was probably thinking about sex. So, MM tried to get the guy directly to other thoughts.

„Just look what you can buy here and leave me alone."

Of course, the attempt was unsuccessful. In search of help MM turned to the saleswoman, who apparently just spoke to her boss. After she hung up, she assured MM that Beatrice was already on her way.

„Can I withdraw somewhere until then?" MM wanted to know from the saleswomen. Nevertheless, the guy answered.

„Sure, old fellow. They have cabins with the best movies you can imagine."

Now he also grinned at MM with a set of teeth that had been in its best days long time ago. Just unbearable. At least, the saleswoman seemed to understand the situation he was in. She turned directly to the man.

„Can I help you Bert?"

„Of course. What kind of private services is this snob talking about? I also want to be treated privately by Beatrice."

„Bert, how many more times should I tell you that this is not a brothel."

She pointed to MM, who still didn't know where to go.

„The gentleman can't open the stainless-steel collar around his neck. You know that Beatrice is pretty good at these things."

With a new awakened interest, the man approached MM. He tried to move his horn-rimmed glasses to get a better view on MMs collar. Additionally, he pinched his eyes, which automatically caused his upper lip to pull up. Again his damaged teeth were exposed.

„I could try it. After all, I used to be a precision mechanic."

„And you're no mechanic now?" MM asked without thinking. The question had just slipped out like that. MM would have preferred to have bitten his tongue. How could he be so stupid to maintain a conversation with this person?

„Oh, that was a long time ago. The company was eventually bought by such a guy and broken down into its individual parts. Then there was the alcohol. Well. I am cursed by fate, but life goes on, doesn't it?"

„You're right."

Again, a guy who was only born to be exploited by others. Did he really think MM would feel any pity for him?

„You should have looked for a new job and that's it."

For this answer, MM got a look that was supposed to tell him that this was clearly the wrong answer. The man began to knock his index finger against MMs chest.

„Now listen carefully, you little snobs. The way you look tells me that you've seen better days. Slave collar made of stainless steel around the neck, ears decorated with fat holes, but a behavior as if you were the boss of the world. In addition, a noble suit, which was certainly very expensive and is now in a state in which you would have thrown it away in former days. Do you think I don't realize what disrespect you are treating me with?"

He looked at MM challenging.

„Let me tell you something snob. With all of my heart I wish that the boss can't open your collar. I would certainly not help you for any money in the world. Anyway, not as long as you act as incredibly arrogant as you do it now!"

To underline his words, he looked at MM with wide opened eyes, then turned around and left the store.

Before MM could relax, the woman from the park happily strolled into the shop.

„Good that you found me. Then let's see if I succeed. It's best to go to the office at the back of my shop."

Without waiting for an answer or making sure MM followed her, Beatrice went ahead. After putting her tool and the large keychain on the table, she sat behind MM to take a closer look at the lock.

„Do you have any idea now where Yvonne could be?"

„I certainly didn't come to talk about my wife. Just do your job. I'm going to pay accordingly and that's it."

„Before I read in the newspaper that an unknown woman's body has been found somewhere, I will in any case inform the police that a friend of mine has disappeared. Your problem, if they want to know why the wife's husband doesn't care so much about it."

„I can assure you that I care, but I have other problems to solve. My wife just has to wait. Nothing will happen to her."

„How can you be so sure? As long as you don't know where she is, everything can happen to her."

„Can't you just do your job and stop talking about my damn wife?"

„I just don't understand that. You are forced to do something and threatened and in the very situation your wife disappears."

MM turned to her and had already opened his mouth to answer when Beatrice rebuked him: „Don't move! How can I investigate this lock when you are fidgeting?"

„Then stop asking me about my wife. The wife-problem, after all, is my business."

Beatrice thought she couldn't trust her ears anymore.

„That is your personal matter? Is Yvonne your private property?"

„That's what you have to say with this weird store. You are living on the money from people that are involved in such perverse things."

„You probably don't know the difference between involuntary and voluntary. However, I am happy to explain this to you by a simple example. The guy who locked this slave collar round your neck didn't ask you about it before. It was therefore involuntary. If it had been a matter of voluntary action, he would have told you beforehand that it has a locking mechanism secured with a time lock. As a result, you could have said that you do not want that."

With that Beatrice put her tool back on the table and started to pack everything back in.

„What are you doing? You're too incapable to open the lock? Is it that?"

206

„You are a real smart guy. Yes, I can't open the lock."

„If this is a time lock, just take the battery out. The thing is certainly built in such a way that it automatically opens in the case of a power failure, right?"

„In general, this should be expected. But this is also built in such a way that you can only get to the battery if you work your way through the neck of the wearer. I suspect you don't really want that."

„But there must be some kind of security mechanism! I can't walk around for the rest of my life with this ugly thing around my neck."

Beatrice leaned back comfortably in her chair.

„Nobody talks about life-long. In general, these time locks can only be set to a maximum of one year. The small batteries don't last much longer anyway."

MM looked at Beatrice stunned. Why did he have to get into such crap?

„What if I get sick or something. There has to be an additional mechanism besides the time lock."

Beatrice made a face as if MM had solved it.

„I agree. You can try to cut the material with an angle grinder. Normally, they don't use hardened steel. But don't come up with the idea that I'm dealing with an angle grinder on your neck."

MM had become pale with the word 'angle grinder' and had put his hands on the collar as if for protection.

„Nothing else?"

„However, there is usually a second possibility."

His expression became an optimistic glance.

„Nowadays, most of those parts have a small receiver. This means that there is a kind of remote control. Works like your TV and stuff like that."

„How do I get it?"

„Actually, not at all. No idea at what frequency this is set. And if you'd know that, you would miss the code that can open the locking mechanism."

„You can probably try that. Do you have something like that in your store?"

„No, of course not. I think that is too dangerous."

„So, my visit was in vain. I'm not a bit further. Stupid bitch. First you tell a big story that you could open all the locks and if a proper task comes up, then you're just a miserable failure."

With that, he left the room and stomped through the store outside. A little moments later, the saleswoman joined her.

„Everything ok with you, boss?"

„All the best Petra. I learned from this idiot everything I wanted to know. And the best thing is that I really was unable to open the lock. I did not have to pretend it."

„Why wouldn't you have done that?"

„Because that's Yvonne's husband and because he cares a shit about what's happening with or to Yvonne."

When she heard this, Petra began to smile,

„Then I'm all the more happy that Bert just did some silly talk with him. You should have seen that. The guy really had a problem to control himself."

***

„Normally I always have to make sure that the blood circulation of all limbs is maintained in my models. But it doesn't matter to you. You've probably already thought about that yourself, right?"

Yvonne couldn't even raise her head to look her tormentor in the eye. She felt painfully every muscle and tendon in her body and was fully focused on not losing balance again. She had no sense of how long she had been standing on the bales of her right foot, but knew that she couldn't stand for much longer. Then she would immediately feel the pull on her neck again. This would bring back the fear that he would suffocate her. The last time he had help her out of that position was after her airways were as good as closed. As punishment for her inattention, however, he had attached even more bondage. Her leg was now, like dance figures of a well-trained ballet

dancer, stretched out on her torso. The foot just pointed up-
wards.

***

As in the past, when she had visited him for regular bondage
sessions, Beatrice parked her car in one of the side streets and
walked the rest of the way across the large forecourt. When
Marc did not respond to the ringing, she carefully pressed
against the large door, which, as she had previously remembered, had not fallen into the lock again. She was determined
not to leave the house before Marc had told her his clients, to
which he had sold one of his collars. Even at first glance at
MMs neck, she felt she knew exactly this type of collar much
better than she liked.

„Marc are you there? It's me, Beatrice!"

She listened into the studio, but couldn't hear anything. Out
of old familiarity with Marc, she went on into the studio and
drew attention to herself by shouting. After a few minutes,
she was sure she was alone. Her original attempt to contact
him via mobile phone had failed. Apparently, he had changed
the number. Even at the fixed-line connection, she had only
been able to leave a message on tape. But now that she finally
had a hot track, she couldn't wait a long time, so she had immediately sat down in her car and now she was standing here.

Just taking a quick look at the office couldn't really hurt.
Eventually, Marc would certainly help her finding the kidnapper. The faster she had the address, the better.

When she heard the fans buzzing, she knew that the PCs
weren't shut down. Automatically she turned on the screens.
On both screens there were rooms of an apartment. The person who ran back and forth in some camera settings was no
one else than MM.

„Holy shit. Seams I made the hit of my life."

It wasn't until she looked more closely at the various camera
settings that she realized that there was another apartment on
the second screen. The whole style of furnishing was

209

completely different. At the same time as realizing that Yvonne might have been detained in this second apartment, she heard a car door slam in the yard. Instead of the expected Marc, she saw the man from the parking lot approaching the studio. She had followed him along with Rondo, but had to give up very quickly, because he had made a safe but highly unauthorized driving maneuver at a motorway entrance. If Rondo would have copied him, he would definitely have been noticed. After all, that's exactly why the man had acted like that.

So now this man went straight to the studio. Beatrice quickly turned off the screens and hid in the adjoining broom chamber, which she knew from earlier, when she had sometimes helped Marc to clean up.

The moment she pulled close the fortunately non-creaking door, the man came to the office and settled on the desk chair. Beatrice could only guess what he was doing, as she could not see anything through the closed door. She hoped he wouldn't come up with the idea of opening the broom chamber.

Just as she was thinking about how best to use the surprise moment if he opened the door, she heard her own voice from the tape:

„Hi Marc, it's Beatrice. I urgently need information from you. I'm pretty sure I saw one of your collars, but it was used completely unerotically in a blackmail and kidnapping case. It has the serial number 183. Please check immediately who bought it. It's really important."

Beatrice was stunned for a brief moment. Then she heard the man's voice.

„What an attentive creature this little Beatrice is after all. Already the short incident in the parking lot has found my pleasure. Now she has also recognized the collar. Really excellent. One can only hope that she does not like to show up here."

After that, there wasn't much to hear for a long time. Apparently, he had a lot of work to do on the PC. Then she finally saw through the crack of the door how the light in the office went out. This was followed by the closing of a door and the barely audible driving away of a car.

After collecting herself for a few seconds, Beatrice opened the door with a jolt and rolled into the room as fast as possible. To her relief, she found that the precautionary acting hadn't been necessary. She really was alone again. In order not to let the light of the screens fall into the night that has now been approached, she closed the curtains and switched on the screens again. On one of them, MM was still visible. On the other, however, an e-mail program was visible. She clicked the recently sent mails.

„*Dear Ladies and Dear Gentlemen,*

I know that your esteemed attention has not escaped the fact that a certain Mr. Müller, better known as MM, has had a considerable number of problems in recent days and weeks. I must freely admit that I was the cause of these problems. A detailed discussion of my motives would certainly go too far now.

I took the liberty to attach a small number of pictures to this mail. Please be so kind to study them with reasonable care. I also strongly recommend to look at the link mentioned at the end of this mail, as here is more material waiting for your expert analysis.

For my part, I have to say goodbye to the game at this point, but I don't want to miss to wish everyone involved a good time."

At the end of the mail she found the promised link. A quick glance was enough for Beatrice to realize that MM would have something to explain to the prosecution.

But now it was only a matter of finding out where Yvonne was being held.

For a while, she searched aimlessly on the computer and hoped to find any clues to the location of the webcams. Eventually she left the screens and turned to the folders in the filing cabinet. But here she found only documents related to the

211

business. When she realized that she wouldn't get any further in this way, she reached for her mobile phone.

„Hello Günther, it's Beatrice. I need your help. There is a hot trace that will lead to the disappearance of Yvonne Müller. But I can't get any further on my own."

Rednich offered her talking the next day, as a pile of incriminating material against MM had just arrived by e-mail.

„I know. That has just been sent off from here. I was kind of witness."

She briefly summarized what had happened and told the address.

In exactly half an hour Rednich would ask her to leave the building. That would be the end of her investigations. Of course, he had asked her not to touch anything, but how should he decide which fingerprints she had left before and which ones she had left after the call. She went to the studio and searched for some places where she would store material that no one else should find.

Just as she was starting the search, she saw the reflections of blue light on the walls. So, the good old Rednich did not trust her and had already sent the uniformed colleagues from the local station as vanguard.

***

„Hallo Mr. Müller."

„What do you want again? I cannot imagine that there is any question that I will answer without the presence of my lawyer."

Smidt and Rednich had not expected any other response.

„That is perfectly fine. Strictly speaking, it is even my duty to point out that a lawyer would be appropriate for you."

She held a paper.

„This paper allows me to put you in the patrol car behind me and take you to the Bureau. You can then inform your lawyer. As it looks like, we have plenty of time to wait for your lawyer to arrive, as we have already prepared a small room with sleeping accommodation for you."

Smidt pointed to the patrol car.

„May I ask you?"

While MM in alternation stared at the warrant and Smidt, his face got completely pale.

„Why? I mean, you just told me that I had nothing to do with the murder of Triebel."

„That's correct" Smidt nodded approvingly. „Does the name Karlsson tell you anything?"

MM didn't know the answer. Denial was certainly completely wrong. There were too many traces. But admit that he had found him dead in front of the hut? Better not. Too many questions. 'Why didn't you inform the police? Or an ambulance? How did you even know that the man was dead? Why were you in the hut? What did Mr. Karlsson want to do out there?'

„Hello! Mr. Müller! You're okay so far?"

MM did not know how long he had been silent. Anyway, so long that even the biggest idiot had to realize that he knew things he didn't want to reveal.

„I don't talk until I've spoken to my lawyer."

„That is your decision. Then may I ask you to go ahead to the car now?"

„I'll just get a few things to wear."

While MM was turning around, he felt the firm grips of the two officers.

„We have enough in stock. Now we are going to the Bureau in first place. Everything else will turn out alright."

MM just needed a few seconds to calm down. Somewhere in his mind he knew that he had lost the game.

„Please let me go alone. I promise to come along. The last thing I need now are neighbors who can gossip about me."

The two officers took a look.

„Ok. We're letting go now. But the next wrong move will mean 'handcuffing'."

MM nodded „okay."

On the way to the Bureau, however, he could no longer hold back.

„Do you seriously accuse me of killing Karlsson?"

„After all, there is much to be said for it, Mr. Müller."

„What exactly, if I may ask?"

„We will talk about all those things later. For the moment I have to ask you to be patient."

MM decided to give up for the moment. He started looking out of the window.

„How do you know Karlsson is dead? We just asked you if the name tells you anything?" Smidt wanted to know.

MM rolled eyes and preferred to remain silent.

***

Instead of Rednich, Hottel, a computer expert, came. He could best be described with the word 'stoned'. He was led into the office and, after he looked at the webcam images, immediately started opening various programs and starting analysis on his laptop. Beatrice had the impression that, within some seconds, he had isolated himself from the outside world.

About an hour later, Rednich, his colleague and a small team of forensic experts arrived. While the forensics started working, Beatrice explained everything again.

After that, she couldn't do anything. As hard as it was, she had no choice but to wait.

***

„So, my dear, then we want to put you in a slightly more comfortable position. You've been going through really well. As a reward, you will get a little break now."

He freed her raised leg from the bondage. Yvonne, who had lost the feeling in her leg in the last few hours, screamed through the gag as her leg fell down without further support. When blood circulation came back to life, it got even worse,

214

as the intense feeling of a thousand needles began. Unfazed by her obvious pain, Jacque finally took the tension out of the chain until Yvonne lay on the floor. For her, this meant even more problems, as now also her arms were flooded with blood again. With the words „we don't want you to get stupid ideas" he attached a chain to her handcuffs and another to her feet. This allowed him to fix her in the middle of the room. Now she could move her arms and legs, but was unable to get her hands up to her head to free herself from the gag.

„Relax. You have a break until tomorrow morning. For the next shooting I need daylight."

He threw another blanket over her and then disappeared into the adjoining room.

It took Yvonne some time to realize the situation. She was still alive and had apparently not yet suffered any permanent damage. The only thing that tormented her now was her wide-spread jaw. Carefully moving her arms and legs had shown her that everything was stiff, but as she put it in her head, it was 'responsive'. She had no idea what time it was. The only thing she knew was that at the moment she didn't see how she could have freed herself. So, she gave in to the need to sleep. When you sleep, she thought, the gag was perhaps more bearable.

Saturday 26th May

„Boss, I found the location of the other webcams."

Hottel had been very relaxed walking to the small bus, which was used as an improvised operations center.

Rednich looked instinctively at the clock. Soon the sun had to rise. In fact, he was used to Hottel getting results faster. Otherwise he would not have spent the night on the uncomfortable bus. When he looked around, he realized that Beatrice had listened to his advice and had distanced herself from the crime scene. At least one who could sleep in her bed that night.

The coordinates that Hottel had for him, pointed to an area that would soon fall victim to lignite surface mining. He estimated the distance to be perhaps 100km. Since there was no immediate danger, he decided to wake up his colleague and go with her without alarming the local police.

When they left the yard, life came to a small car in one of the side streets. Beatrice had been awake all night. It was clear to her that she didn't even have to ask Rednich if she could come along if the address was found. By the time he sent her home, her decision to hang on to his car had already been made. Either she managed to stay on or she didn't. At least she wanted to try.

The journey went directly towards the motorway. So, since there wasn't a lot of traffic anyway, she could fall back a little bit and trust that she would know which driveway he would take.

On the highway, Rednich finally accelerated. It was clear to Beatrice that his BMW was clearly superior to her car, but on the other hand, on German motorways you can't always drive any speed. Even at night. Since it was no case that would have allowed flashing blue light according to the official rules, this was not used by Rednich. That's how he was. Always good within the framework of the regulations. For Beatrice, this was the opportunity to catch up with him again and again. The only thing she couldn't always make sure was whether she followed the right pair of lights.

When he finally left the highway, she got quite close. To her relief she could see, that she was still following the right car.

As they drove on a county road, dawn was rising. This would put an end to the pursuit very soon. On the one hand, she was able to identify Rednich better, but on the other hand she was also more present for Rednich. She wasn't an anonymous headlight in the rearview mirror anymore. Thus, it was easy for him to identify.

While she was still following her thoughts, he changed to an even smaller road. As far as she could follow the signs, they were in a rather rural area. So, it was to be assumed that the journey was about to end. They drove to a village that seemed completely deserted. Since no one could be seen, Beatrice decided to wait and see which direction Rednich would continue. She had to disappear completely from his rearview mirror. A short time later, she saw him on a narrow road that led up a slope. If she followed him now, she could also push down the horn button. It was completely impossible to stay hidden there.

She decided to park the car and look around the small village. At first glance, it seemed that the village really was deserted. Some doors and windows were even nailed. But other houses still looked inhabited. In front of her spiritual eye, she saw old people sitting behind the windows who didn't really know how to live the rest of their life in this loneliness.

At the road there was a farm, which was apparently still managed. At least there was an old tractor in the yard and an opened barn gate behind which some equipment was hiding. It was only when she had walked a few meters further that she realized that she had not only seen agricultural equipment in the barn. In one corner were tripods and even headlights, as used by professional photographers. She quickly walked back and looked into the barn again. In fact. All the objects she had seen again and again with Marc in the sessions. What did the stuff do here? Rednich had been directed to a location near the village?

She watched the house for a few breaths and when she could not see any movement, she quickly made the short way across the yard to the barn. Even before she could take a closer look at the parts, she heard steps. In the back wall of the barn was a door. That was the place where the person had to approach in between the next seconds. Beatrice quickly hid behind a support column. If she was lucky, the person would pass her a few meters away without discovering her.

In fact, it sounded like someone was approaching the photo equipment. She heard the rattling of the equipment that arises during lifting. After that, the steps moved away, sounding a little more irregular. Apparently, the person dragged the equipment outside. A quick glance showed Beatrice that some parts were still in the barn. Near the door stood a mighty old tractor, which probably had been built several decades ago. A much better hiding place. From there, she could also take a look at the person who apparently wanted to take a few photos. When Beatrice took a position there, she realized that she could also look into the backyard through the open door.

What she saw, however, left her in shock. A woman's body hung on a frame above the meadow. The woman was attached to the corners of the frame with her hands and feet, so that she hung in the horizontal with her legs and arms wide open. In addition, the head was tied in a way that she had to put it in her neck. Thus, she looked parallel across the ground to the horizon. It probably didn't work with the sight, as she was wearing a blindfold. Beatrice didn't need a second look to recognize Yvonne. And the photographer was actually none other than Marc.

Just as Beatrice was picking up her mobile phone to order Rednich, Marc turned back to the barn. He said goodbye to Yvonne with the words:

„Unfortunately, I still have to wait an hour with the photo. The sun is not yet high enough. Time enough to pick up a few buns. Don't run away."

Yvonne only made a grunt in response. Afterwards Marc passed Beatrice's hiding place and left the yard in an old van.

The opportunity was unique. Beatrice ran to Yvonne.

„Yvonne, It's me. Stay calm. I'll loosen the bondage and then we get off."

First, she opened the blindfold so let Yvonne's eyes adjust to the light again. As soon as the two had eye contact, Yvonne started grunting again. Beatrice opened the gag and pulled it out of her mouth. She saw from the panic in Yvonne's eyes that the far too big gag has been in her mouth for too long. The jaw muscles would take a while to get back to their normal state.

„Don't worry. When you're safe, we'll let warm water rins over your muscles and you'll see that it's all right again"

Beatrice tried to reassure her friend with these words, but Yvonne got even more restless. The moment Beatrice noticed that Yvonne was looking past her, she saw the shadow beside her. Instinctively, Beatrice rolled to the side in the fall. Next to her, a heavy object hit the ground.

Marc had come back and had just tried to kill her with a pickaxe. Beatrice was quickly back on her feet, but even faster Marc had put both hands around Yvonne's neck.

„Stay where you are, otherwise I have to push her larynx inwards."

Beatrice estimated the distance. At least two steps were necessary to put him out of action with a professional kick. Clearly too much. Marc made an extremely attentive impression. Though it was unlikely that he could kill Yvonne within a split second, it would surely be enough time to change his position. Too dangerous.

„I think you're picking up buns?"

A smirk came on his face.

„I wanted to. But you were so stupid to park your car clearly visible. Then I thought: Better see if somebody came to visit me. And, surprise, surprise, dear Beatrice came for a final photo session."

„After hitting me with the device there, I wouldn't have been very cooperating, Marc."

A calculating smile was on his face.

219

„But now that you're still so unharmed..."

„You're completely crazy? Are you seriously thinking I'm letting you photoshoot me?"

Beatrice instinctively took a step back.

„No, I don't think so. But who knows what you are willing to do when this lady her stops breathing from time to time?"

He gave Yvonne's head a slight jolt, so that she swung with the entire frame, which was attached to only one chain. With one single step Marc positioned Yvonne between himself and Beatrice. Much to Beatrice' frustration she had to realize that he was quite safe now.

„What do you think of starting to undress slowly?"

To confirm the question, he gave Yvonne a sharp slap. As he held the frame, Yvonne screamed after taking the whole force.

„You can scream as much as you want. There is no human soul left in the whole village. All gone."

As he raised the other hand, he looked challengingly at Beatrice.

„Okay, wait. You convinced me."

To calm him down, she let her jacket slide to the ground.

„Where do you want to start my bondage? The frame is quite nice. But it only offers space for one person."

„Stop this senseless small talk, otherwise your dear Yvonne lies right here in the grass without ever being able to stand up again. The frame would be free for you."

Beatrice slowly moved on as she desperately searched a solution. She knew that the moment she was going to wear the first shackle, she had lost. The only chance was that Rednich would come back as soon as possible and, like Marc, find her car. But even then, she was far from being saved. After all, Rednich would have no reason to walk straight to the meadow in the backyard of the farm.

Still, she couldn't think of anything better. She had to be so slow that as much time as possible came out and she had to be fast enough that he wouldn't hurt Yvonne any further.

„Do you think I'll let you spoil me all morning?" Marc wanted to know. Yvonne had to receive the next slap.

„I'm already doing it. Now just leave her alone. In former times you used to be much more relaxed, when I undressed."

„I used to be the shy gay photographer" was his answer while using his former intonation.

When Beatrice finally stood naked in front of him, he threw handcuffs to her.

„Chain yourself to the frame. Between her feet."

Without a saving idea, Beatrice had the first opening snapped around her right wrist and wanted to attach the second end to the frame.

„Stop. Not that way. The second end comes to your other hand. The chain is inside the frame. Got it?"

When Beatrice hesitated, he grabbed Yvonne by her still opened mouth.

„Look here. Poor Yvonne still cannot close the mouth. Do you want to be blamed if I put the gag back at her? This certainly hurts a lot."

With played concern, he looked at Beatrice. Just as she was about to have the handcuffs finally snapped, his face distorted. At the same time, he tried to pull the hand back from Yvonne's mouth, pulling the entire frame away from Beatrice. It was immediately clear to Beatrice that Yvonne must have bitten. Beatrice went into the squat and shot as fast as she could under the frame on Marc's legs. Her plan was to pull them off with her shoulder and hope that would be enough to bring him down. After that, all she could hope for was that he couldn't recover fast enough.

Marc, who was still helpless in front of Yvonne, had no time to realize Beatrice' plan. He was completely blocked by the pain his thumb sent out. Should he push Yvonne away with his free hand? Probably the pain would then become even greater. The most important thing was to get as little tension as possible on his thumb.

He only noticed Beatrice's rushing shoulder when it landed precisely in his testicles. He went to his knees in a whining and finally got free from Yvonne's mouth.

Beatrice could hardly believe the rapid change in the situation. Marc lay in front of her in embryo position and apparently did not know whether the injury to the thumb or his testicles created the worse pain. Desperately, he covered his thumb with his free hand and was still completely occupied with himself.

For Beatrice, it was clear that this situation could not last forever. She looked around, took one of the ropes lying around, made a wide loop at one end and pulled it over his foot. Before Marc was able to react, she jumped a few steps back to tighten the loop. Now she was able to drag him slowly through the entire field all day long without giving him a single chance of escape. When she looked into his eyes, she knew that he had understood.

With this realization, his pain caught up with him again. For Beatrice, the only task left was to free Yvonne as quickly as possible. The way she hung in the frame couldn't be good in the long run. Marc didn't seem to be capable of big action at the moment. Nevertheless, she could not afford to be reckless. If he would win the upper hand again, she would certainly have no chance. Keeping the rope tight she slowly went to Yvonne.

„Yvonne. You keep a close eye on him as soon as he moves, you scream! Got me?"

Yvonne, who was busy cleaning her mouth as best she could with her own spit, nodded approvingly. She immediately stopped trying to give an answer. Talking still wasn't an option.

Beatrice began to free her feet, then her head and finally her hands from the shackles.

During the action Marc had started to whimper more and more.

„She has bitten my thumb off. I'm bleeding to death. You have to dress the wound."

Beatrice was not in the mood to feel pity for him. She looked at Yvonne. She shrugged her shoulders and then pointed to a spot where something indefinable lay.

Beatrice quickly re-dressed, attached Marc with some additional ropes as tightly as possible to the frame. Then she decided to first bring Yvonne to safety. On the way through the barn, she took an old blanket, which she threw over Yvonnes shoulders.

As they stepped out into the street, they ran straight into Rednich and his colleague's arms. While Smidt called for reinforcements and the emergency doctor, Rednich took Yvonne from Beatrice and escorted her to his car.

„What about the kidnapper?"

„Behind the yard. I tied him up. He might have a serious injury to his genitals and a deep bite wound to his thumb. Presumably, he will be out of action for a while. I wanted to get Yvonne to safety first."

„Was he armed?"

„No idea. He attacked me with a pickaxe. But it may well be that he also has real weapons in the house."

The two officers communicated with a glance.

„You handle her alone, Beatrice?" Rednich wanted to know. Before she could signal 'no problem' they heard the first siren together with a shot that was fired not far away.

„Attention!"

They quickly hid to safety in a doorway.

„Where did it come from?"

They had not noticed any damage to the car or any of the surrounding houses.

„No idea."

„Can he get away from the backyard on another path, Beatrice?"

„Don't know." After a short pause, she added „Yeah, for sure. It was surrounded by no walls. If Marc can run, contrary to my guess, he can be gone in all sorts of directions."

„Shit."

A few minutes of attention followed. The all-clear signal came when the colleagues arrived and a protected team could be sent into the yard. The team found Marc with a head shot at the spot Beatrice had previously described.

***

„MM, that looks damn bad. Your fingerprints on the suspected murder weapon, your fingerprints on the car. Your genetic fingerprints in the car…"

These were the words MM did not want to hear from his lawyer.

„Listen, I was trapped by a blackmailer. Probably all the time he wanted nothing more than to blame any murders on me. This whole traveling around was just a little extra joke for him. Find the connection to my old deals. I have looked for them by myself and am sure that not only one, but directly several of the old files are missing. Maybe people conspired against me."

The lawyer leaned back with slight resignation.

„How do you imagine that? To be clear, these files relate exclusively to illegal business, don't they?"

MM nodded and continued the lawyer's idea.

„And the particularly explosive parts of it lay in the safe."

„You did not deposit the documents from the safe somewhere with the notary in dozens of copies, but kept them at your home without any copy?"

„Of course. How else? Should I show them around in the neighborhood? Look, I've fooled a bunch of stupid idiots and here's the incriminating material. Wasn't exactly legal."

„Why did you keep the documents in the first place?"

As MM raised his hands resignedly the lawyer suggested:

„As a means of blackmail, if someone thinks otherwise?"

„Of course. Otherwise, the idiots or at least some of them can knock on my door at any time and try to turn the tables."

„Have you ever heard of fires?" When he saw the questioning look of MM, he continued. „What would you have done

if your stall had just been burned off? Some stupid short cir-
cuit current or something."

„The safe was, of course, fireproof."

„With built-in refrigerator or what?" The lawyer waved.

„We don't have to argue now. What happened, happened.
If you don't have copies, I can't do anything as long as you
can't give me any clues from your memory and even then, we
would have to prove that it was one of them. So, think carefully about how we want to proceed. Consider whether you
have enough facts in your memory to go in that direction at
all. Also keep in mind that in your opinion, these are all just
idiots. The question, then, is whether any of them is even able
to do such a thing. Even if you succeed and find the bloke,
you gathered enough material to be accused for committing
economic crimes. Yeah, that's really a trap."

Epilog

On the beach, an elderly man sat in a street café. He had just managed to gain access to the Internet – of course as incognito as possible - in order to finally send his last message.

„Dear Yvonne,

I have to apologize. Unfortunately, my assistant had gotten out of control. Luckily, smart Beatrice was there in time to free you.

To my great shame, I must confess that I was a few minutes late. In this respect, please send my sincere thanks to Beatrice.

After you had moved back to the front part of the estate, I had a few minutes to punish the unfaithful assistant and then say goodbye to the game. I wish you all the best.

As it was published in the newspaper, MM has been 'withdrawn from service' as I would like to express. At least for a few years. It would be a lie if I would phrase something about regrets. Yes, I'm happy about it. This was intended to be one of the possible final chapters of the whole action."

He read the writing again and, after some hesitation, added:

„ You're probably wondering why I did all this? The answer is actually quite simple. Twenty years ago, I handed over my well-run company to my son. MM has gotten it out of my son using nasty tricks. Since I hadn't extracted my money yet, me and my son were suddenly poor people. MM felt very entertained. My son could not cope with this. He committed suicide.

But I could cope with it out of one single reason: A proper revenge.

When I finally knew how to do it, chance came to my aid. As suddenly as I had lost my fortune before, I won it back thanks to gambling. Now I had this pleasant motivating tool, called money, at my disposal with which I could get some useful assistants on board.

You know the rest of the story."

He moved the mouse to the send-button. When he remembered that most of the ingenious offenders were caught because they ended up having the insatiable desire to tell the world how brilliant they are, his index finger stuck above the left mouse key.

Acknowledgements and thinks like that

Of course, I would like to thank all those who have supported me in writing this story, but especially I thank my imagination.

The biggest headache I had, was the choice of names. No idea how the other writing people get the names of their actors. So, if you are named like a person in this story, be assured that it was not my intention.

If there is anyone who thinks she/he recognizes other stories in this book, I assure you that I don't know that story. Everything I wrote comes from my imagination. With quite a few of the passages told, I would very much like to hope that they can happen only in the imagination and that in reality they would fail because of the many unpredictable imponderables that life entails.